HEATHER BOYD

Once a Husband

HUNT CLUB – 6

Acknowledgements

I would like to thank my editor, Kelli, for her outstanding help and support in creating this book.

I am also eternally grateful to the fans of the Hunt Club series who wrote and asked for Angelo's story to be told. Hope you enjoy!

By Heather Boyd

Almost an Equal
Barely a Master
Hardly a Stranger

Just a Dream
Never a Gentleman
Once a Husband

Prologue

1814 London

The carriage rolled to a stop and Rupert Manning, Lord Bracknell, peered out through the rain at the establishment owned by his father, the Duke of Staines. The Hunt Club was something of a mystery to him and he did not like the implications of this visit. He scowled at his father's servant, Redding, to disguise his uneasiness. "Why the rear entrance?"

"His Grace's orders, my lord. He wanted you to see everything else before the patrons know you are admitted to the club." Redding leaned a little closer than Rupert found comfortable. "Since you have no idea what goes on, and society is aware you are not a member, you can greet everyone later with all the facts in your possession. His Grace did not want you to be uncomfortable."

Too little, too late. "And he didn't think that would have already been the case? I've had dozens of lords smirking at my ignorance for years."

If only this could be a bad dream.

He was ushered inside and led to a small room containing only a desk that held a book, pen and ink upon it.

Redding flipped open the book. "If you could just sign the register, my lord, we can then proceed upstairs."

"A register?" He was a duke's son, and now the bloody caretaker of the place in his father's stead. The old man was asking too much of him. He clenched his jaw.

Redding sighed. "No one is allowed beyond this chamber without signing."

He flipped the pages to the first and pointed at the duke's name, his own name, the dukes of Byworth and Lewes, and onward down a list of the most influential lords of the realm.

Rupert's jaw dropped in surprise. He'd had no idea what sort of men would frequent his father's club, but if the Duke of Byworth, a man he deeply respected, was a member, then surely it couldn't be too bad. He signed his name and stood back.

Redding snapped the book shut and shoved it under his arm, now all business and brisk efficiency as he led the way. "There are twenty-three rooms within the house. The great room and gallery, dining room and library on the lower level, but above stairs is where the club differs from most others. Here a lord can find pleasure of every sort imaginable, and some I don't understand at all." He pointed along a narrow corridor. "Patrons come through there from the front rooms and into this reception chamber."

Rupert nodded, attempting to imagine the place full of people. Given the size of the space he assumed it was well patronized. He turned as a flash of red caught his eye, discovering a woman moving about the rooms. She moved toward them, skirts swishing provocatively about her legs. Her dark hair was swept up behind her head but her face was a thing of beauty. Thick dark lashes framed her eyes under delicately curved brows and her olive complexion was flawless.

"Redding, so good to see you, darling," she said, her voice husky and rough. "Who is this fine gentleman? I must make his acquaintance."

Rupert couldn't look away. The red gown wasn't daring or provocative but he was utterly transfixed by her very presence, and could do no more than nod while the introductions were being made.

The woman slipped her arm through his and stared at him too. "So, you have come to us at last. I had begun to fear the duke would never relent and keep you from us indefinitely. We are, of course, at your complete disposal."

"Thank you," he murmured, appreciating this unexpected development. The woman appeared quite a cut above the rest.

Redding scowled at her. "Marinari, remember the duke's rules."

She merely smiled. "Every rule can be broken."

Rupert did not necessarily agree but he began the tour with Marinari as his guide, Redding trailing after them silently. After ten minutes, he realized he'd never been flirted with quite so much in his entire life. As far as the day went, it was certainly proving interesting. He was extremely flattered too.

He couldn't help but stare as a young man stumbled from a bedchamber, hair in disarray, clothed far too casually for this time of morning, and a well-dressed man followed. The second man blew the younger one a kiss of farewell.

Redding cleared his throat and spoke in a tone that brooked no disobedience. "Marinari, would you excuse us?"

Marinari withdrew. Rupert allowed Redding to lead him into another chamber and close the door. "The club caters to many tastes, my lord. There are an equal number of ladies and fellows available in the club for pleasure."

He froze in shock. So there were more men with his father and Redding's taste for depravity here. "Was my surprise that obvious?"

Clearly it was. He crossed the room, pulled open a wardrobe and scanned the contents until his face cooled. He would never understand how his father could want to kiss a man, let alone Redding.

"I'm afraid so. There is worse to come. I didn't feel right not warning you."

At least Redding was not laughing at him. "I always wondered why my father kept you around so much. Seems he couldn't risk letting you go. The things you could say, heh?" He stared at the shoes sitting empty at the bottom of the cupboard, noting their ridiculously large size. Apparently, there were also giant women in the club. Unless...

He swallowed. "Redding, why are the ladies' slippers so large?"

Redding peered around his shoulder. "Those clothes do not belong to the whores here. They are garments and fripperies for the members to slip on if they enjoy that sort of thing."

He slammed the doors closed in horror. "I'm in a mad house."

"One can grow accustomed to madness."

"What exactly is your position with my father?" He turned, unable to keep his questions to himself another moment. "You are certainly more than a mere footman to him."

Redding shuffled his feet. "I joined the duke's household at age ten. Your grandsire preferred him to be always attended by servants, so I was added to their number to provide companionship while he prowled the estate."

Rupert remembered Redding always being around but, as with most servants, he'd never considered when he had arrived.

"Over time, when he'd grown surer of himself and stood up to his family's strictures, your father dismissed the others and kept me exclusively."

He nodded as he recalled Redding was the one servant in his father's employ whom had been a constant presence in his life when he was growing up and until now. "I have a vague memory of you, from when I was a boy, standing behind my father in the driving rain beside my mother's grave not long after she was laid to rest."

Redding winced. "He grieved for her more than you know."

Anger stirred in him unexpectedly. "Is that why he sent me away? Why I didn't see him for almost a year?"

Redding raked his hand through his hair. "There is much more to see, my lord, if you would just come this way."

He studied the grim set of Redding's features carefully, realizing he wouldn't get the answers he wanted from this man. Redding was a loyal servant. The duke's man through and through, apparently.

He followed Redding into the next room and he stared around in confusion. There were chairs with ropes and buckled straps. He would not dare to sit in any one of them. They looked damned uncomfortable.

"Everything is cleaned and oiled daily. You may touch anything you're curious about."

He slowly circled the room, turning several dials on one device. He narrowed his eyes at what that did to the contraption. If a person were to sit on this, then his legs would open wide. He gasped softly in shock. He was in hell. Absolutely in hell.

No wonder his father's friends had been laughing at his ignorance of this club.

He peeked at the man across the room. Redding relaxed against the door as if a contraption like this was as mundane as a child's rocking horse. Rupert nudged the seat, and it swayed in a similar fashion to the toy too.

He cleared his throat, unnerved by the idea of his father in this room. "How many of the members would use this chamber?"

"Quite a few." Redding met his gaze directly. "More than half. But that wasn't your real question, was it?"

He shook his head and braced himself.

Redding grimaced. "Your father has never used this chamber to my knowledge, or sought the entertainment among those he employs here. He has found his pleasures elsewhere since the club began. He's said more than once that a landlord should not piss in his own parlor, so to speak, unless he wanted trouble. The place is an investment to him. One he takes great pains to manage well. The whores are clean and biddable, violence is frowned upon, and those working here are paid a decent wage with adequate comforts for their labors. He would want that to continue."

"He doesn't dabble here because he has you?" Rupert shot back.

"He has preferred gentlemen and ladies of his own rank."

He wouldn't put much past his father now, so he asked the obvious question. "At the same time?"

Redding didn't answer, and that spoke volumes about his father peccadillos. What did Redding think? Was he as unaffected by all of this as he appeared?

The silence lengthened and a flush of color swept up Redding's cheeks in a way that proved he didn't approve of either the situation or the question. Was Redding jealous that his father kissed others?

He laughed at the very idea. "I have to hand it to my father. He certainly keeps his secrets well and truly hidden. I find I am amazed you've put up with him for so long, Red."

As he was speaking, he felt a stab of pity for this servant. It was a miracle he'd stayed in his father's employ for so long, given all this depravity. He slapped his shoulder and stepped out into the hall.

Marinari peeked at him from a nearby room and smiled. Rupert moved toward her when beckoned and was pulled into the room. He didn't know her but he felt drawn to her just the same. "Is everything always so complicated here?"

Her fingers trailed down his shirtfront. "Everything can be very simple, if you keep an open mind."

"That might be impossible."

"We each choose what we show the world." Her hand rose to his face and she gently stroked over his stubble. "Yours is a strong face. A man of character."

"Thank you." Although he shouldn't, he leaned closer, drawn in by the scent of her perfume. Unfortunately, his vision blurred, and instead of reaching for his spectacles, he smiled. "You are beautiful."

She fluttered her lashes and, after a moment of hesitation, captured his lips in a fierce kiss.

Utter shock transfixed him. His lips tingled and when she angled her head, he couldn't help but part his lips. She deepened the kiss, and then his head spun as she turned him against the wall so hard a picture rattled. Marinari kissed him again, and although he fought to gain the upper hand, he could not dislodge her.

He must tell her he was a married man, but he'd never been so determinedly pursued in his life. What man in his right mind could immediately resist the temptation of a woman seducing him?

Her fingers dug into his hips and pressed him against her body. He groaned as the tingling in his lips spread throughout his entire body. It was as if lightning flooded his skin with dangerous sensations. He held Marinari to him, reveling in that feeling.

They rocked against each other, devouring each other with deep kisses. Marinari bit his lip. He drew back a little, capturing her gaze. The dark brown orbs burned with a wild desire unlike anything he'd ever seen before. In response, he ran his hand down her side, sliding over her derriere, and drew up her gown a little.

Her brow rose as if daring him and he jerked the fabric up higher. Hard thighs greeted him. He lifted her leg around his own to fit himself to her and kissed her deeply while he rubbed against her sex with his cock.

He broke the kiss suddenly as he registered a presence between them.

Hardness where none but his should be.

Heart pounding, he eased her away and thrust a hand under her skirts, directly over her sex.

Her cock burned his palm. Long, hard and hot.

To be certain, he moved his fist upward and brushed his thumb over the top. Seed leaked from the tip.

Marinari groaned. "That's so good. Stroke me again."

Rupert recoiled. "What the hell are you?"

She winked. "Exactly what you need."

"You're a man?" Rupert's face flamed. "You deceived me!"

After all the shocks of today, he couldn't think beyond the need to strike out. He threw a fist at the fellow's smirking face.

The man caught him, and Rupert screamed as pain zinged up his limb. He fell to his knees, caught in a hold that looked deceptively easy yet caused tears to fill his eyes.

"That was impolite," the man chided.

"Don't call me that," he hissed.

"Why not? Surely your intentions are honorable."

"Are you mad? Everyone is suddenly mad. For God's sake, I'm a married man. I have normal desires."

"And yet you stroked my cock so perfectly, I know you've experienced such illicit passions before."

Rupert's stomach rolled as an old memory, one he'd banished since his school days, returned. "That's a lie."

Marinari clucked her—his—tongue. "And such a kiss as I've never experienced before too. Admit it, you desire me, my lord."

"I certainly do not now."

Her brow rose. "Then your impatient cock has a mind of its own."

He didn't need to see. He was still hard. Hard and panting on his knees before a man who wore gowns and hid his gender beneath them. He struggled to stand, to peer at her again, and thankfully Marinari released him. He shook his fist because it had become numb. He marched toward the door. "This isn't over."

"I certainly hope not, Bella. I look forward to our next encounter very eagerly."

Rupert slammed the door behind him and struggled for composure. He failed utterly and, as Redding hurried toward him, he couldn't keep quiet. "She's a bloody man."

"Oh, hell," Redding said, his wince revealing it wasn't that much of a secret around here. "There was one more matter, my lord."

CHAPTER ONE

London
Years later

They say death is peaceful.

Dying certainly is not.

"Help me!"

The man perched on the window ledge of Wiggan's Boarding House shrugged and stared at his dripping hand. Of all the fruits on display at the market, oranges might just be his favorite to steal and to eat as another murky day of life began. He bit into the firm flesh of one and let the juice linger on his lips before dabbing at them with a linen napkin.

"Please," the voice wailed from below in the filthy yard.

"Seven Dials is no place for mercy or kindness," he whispered.

The man missed the berries of home with a sudden and unexpected pang of homesickness. Sun-warmed and ripe straight from the kitchen garden of his family's villa. He'd once gorged on fruit with his innocent younger brothers and sisters. In those carefree days, being first to the table was all he had cared about, and it was that misty memory he clung to now when the world was so bleak and cold. The air was cleaner in that faraway memory, too, than the soot and filth that filled the metropolis of London of his present. He supposed he could have returned to the place of his birth years ago, but even if he was able to make the voyage, what was the point? He'd nothing to return to.

Nothing here either, for that matter, so he made no effort to change his situation. Everyone he'd known and loved there was dust.

"No, don't!"

The gentleman dug in his pocket and found the fruit-studded bun he's stolen on his way back from taking in the sights and sounds of another London night, and inhaled reverently.

The simple things in life were the best—to breathe, to eat, and make as much mischief as he possibly could.

He bit into the bun—and then spat out a small pebble that grated on his teeth. He stared at it in disappointment. He'd had such high hopes when he'd taken it.

He really missed cooks who could cook.

Friends who were real friends.

Lovers who were…*willing* to be with *him* in any guise.

The gentleman scrubbed his hand through his hair, still surprised that he ran short of length after only a brief caress of his head after so many years. It was also an infrequent shock that he barely recognized himself when he saw his own reflection, which meant any past cooks, friends or lovers may not know him if he was standing right in front of them.

"Someone help me!"

He tore off another chuck then ate the soft center first, scraping away the edible portion with his teeth, taking every pleasure from what he put into his body.

He had learned long ago that what little joy could be found in life was taken anywhere and at any time. He glanced about his tiny attic chamber—at his narrow bed, locker of clothes beneath, and a single precious volume of poetry stolen from a bookseller yesterday.

He was content for now.

He was at peace.

He wiped his hands carefully then brushed crumbs off his breeches, resigned that his shabby appearance was utterly necessary. He'd never be welcomed at his favorite shops as he appeared now. He sniffed, and then wrinkled his nose with distaste. He definitely needed a bath soon, too, but in his line of work, cleanliness most often led to suspicion.

"Where ya going, ya pitiful bastard?" a man jeered beneath him, and then a scream tore out of the victim's throat.

He glanced out his window, peering down on a scene he'd viewed many times before. "Amateurs," he complained.

He uncurled the wire-and-bead garrote from beneath the stocking on his left ankle and stretched the length before him. The perfect length to silence any victim. A pity the practice of using them had fallen into disrepute in recent years. Too many liked to play with their prey, making them suffer unduly. Killing with a garrote was elegant, fast and blessedly silent in comparison to the callous violence offered below.

He was grateful for the shadows, but his experience filled in the gaps. There'd be enough claret spilled about down there by now to cover his bed. "So unnecessarily untidy," he muttered with disgust.

There were other sounds that would make a more delicate man shudder.

"Never gamble with your life," he advised when the man below came into view, attempting to crawl away one-armed from the larger man following behind and taunting him. "And always know a way out. If there is no escape possible, make them pay dearly for their insolence."

He sighed. He'd never lost a fight since turning sixteen, which was why he'd done so well as an assassin.

But he was dead to everyone he knew, or was supposed to be. An unmissed and unlamented casualty of war.

He scowled at the turn of his thoughts. "Must be the mild weather making me grim."

The past was an unpleasant memory. Being shot by a man he'd foolishly trusted had given him ample reason to feel put out. Shot, left for dead, nearly damaged beyond fixing, and cast aside like an overflowing night soil pot.

It was enough to make any man irritable, let alone one who could break a neck without breaking a sweat.

His former friend's shot to the shoulder may have been wide of his target, but it was to the point. His services were no longer required and his usefulness had come to an immediate end five years ago on the dark southern coast. His friend had been given orders to kill, and he'd obeyed, appearing pained to do it.

To this day, he continued to live in the shadows, avoiding the streets he used to sneak through with his many unsavory accomplices.

In the yard below, the man was still crawling on his belly, moving toward the blind alley, dragging his legs behind him as if they no longer worked. They were probably broken, and by the way he called out, weaker now and pained, his chest had damage too.

He knew the signs of imminent death as well as anyone in his profession.

The sounds would stop soon, and there would be another body floating in the Thames. Whether the fellow could swim or not made no difference to his chances of avoiding that fate.

He was as good as dead the moment he'd set foot here.

The sounds from below cut off abruptly, and he sighed with relief that it was finally over.

Another fool dead by his own foolishness, but there would always be another.

His meal finished, Angelo Marinari, former assassin, former abbess of the Hunt Club and admirer of fine gowns only women could wear, closed the window on the scene below. It wasn't his business to save the foolish from danger. Not anymore. He was alone, and that was the way he wanted it.

CHAPTER TWO

Never let a man near your throat unless you trust him with your life.

Rupert had never been a careless man by nature, so he reached out to accept the razor from the valet with an impatient flick of his wrist. Although once accustomed to having his every need catered to by servants, he chose to shave himself that night.

He'd been given that piece of parting advice from a man who'd never shown his true face to the world, and it had stuck with him to this day. Trust had to be earned.

He had other small gems of wisdom to cling to when he was out of sorts, but that last seemed the most appropriate at this present time in his life.

His valet reluctantly handed the implement over, and then stood back, eyeing him in slight disapproval as he began to shave himself in the mirror.

"Is there anything else I may do for you this evening, Lord Bracknell?"

Rupert dragged the sharp blade down his face, removing the dark stubble and making quick work of the task. He washed off the remaining soap and checked his reflection, dabbing at a bit clinging near his ear. "No thank you. You may go off and aid Sanderson now."

His brother-in-law, Elwin Sanderson, had dismissed his own valet just yesterday so for now, Rupert's man had a double duty to fill, unfortunately.

Always value loyalty.

Rupert flicked Smith a coin to sweeten his evening and gestured to the door.

When the door closed behind Smith, Rupert let out a sigh. His hapless brother-in-law, who had come to stay for a month and somehow extended his visit by four years at his wife's insistence, was becoming a pain in his backside the way he discarded good servants for imagined failings on their part.

But like many ladies of the *ton*, his wife had overlooked problems at home for more pleasurable diversions such as parties and friends that took her away from their son.

Although disappointed in her desertion of the child, Rupert accepted that his wife lacked a strong bond with their son. She did not pursue any of Rupert's attention either, for that matter. She had been cold to him almost since the day she'd given him an heir, but by all reports, Sally warmed to many other men, and she set her sights on flirting with them publicly.

He glanced toward the doorway to her bedchamber. He didn't bother to test anymore that it was locked against him. He'd endured enough humiliation in that direction to last him a lifetime. "I wonder whose bed you're warming tonight?"

Not that he could be surprised anymore. The gossip was subtle, but of late he'd heard enough to understand they were finished as man and wife. He'd given up hope that his marriage could be salvaged. Sally never sought his company and he had other concerns to fill his days.

He had a son to raise—Charles had just turned four—and he had responsibilities to his estate and the family at large.

Rupert had become decidedly possessive about his time and the interruptions he was prepared to accept. In recent years, so much responsibility had fallen on his shoulders and all of it would eventually fall to his son.

Then there was the Hunt Club to manage, a haven of salacious vice and corruption for his father's cronies—and a constant source of frustration in his life.

He rubbed the back of his neck, disturbing the relic of a past friendship hanging there that he'd never been able to set aside. He'd last seen Angelo Marinari at the club, boldly strolling out the front door on the arm of another man, never to return.

He was said to be dead, killed while protecting

England. Murdered by order of his superiors when he'd outlived his usefulness.

He fingered the beads briefly, wishing that it wasn't the case. He still expected the man who had interrupted his well-ordered life and then vanished without a trace would boldly stroll back through the Hunt Club door one day and upset his world again.

The hope he'd clung to that Marinari had somehow survived being shot had slowly faded until, after five years, he'd begun to mourn the mad bastard. Marinari had been an unusual man in every respect. He'd dressed as a woman when they'd first met and had flirted nonstop at every opportunity thereafter. Rupert didn't entirely trust him to behave when they were alone, but his advice had proven to be sound, and to Rupert's advantage to listen to once upon a time. Rupert had managed to overlook Marinari's choice of feminine fashions for the sake of efficiency in the running of the club. He had been as unnatural a man as any gentleman who frequented the Hunt Club's scandalous rooms.

To his surprise, he missed Angelo Marinari very much.

But Marinari was dead and he had to accept it.

Or so the man who killed him claimed he should.

Yet Rupert had never quite trusted Lord Beecroft's word on Marinari's fate. He'd seen the uncertainty, doubt, filling the earl's eyes as he'd made his confession. There was a chance Angelo lived. Slim, but unlikely.

Angelo hadn't made himself known to Rupert yet after all these years. He had not returned to the club, to London, and it was time to accept that the man must be gone. All he had left was a rosary, and those odd warnings he clung to. They helped him decide how to live.

He scooped up his neckcloth and focused on the task of tying a respectable knot over the shirt and rosary, finding solace in the routine activity. Once he was done, he checked his handiwork before slipping into his evening coat of dull brown.

You stand out in a crowd if you dress to be

remembered.

He was not interested in turning heads. He hardly cared what anyone thought of his presence, so he took Angelo's advice to heart and dressed soberly. The Dunhill Soiree was bound to be a crush tonight, but he'd promised to attend weeks ago and couldn't get out of it now without giving offence to the hosts. If he didn't stand out, he might just be able to leave early without Lord Dunhill being any the wiser. Maybe he could also slip away from Sanderson in the process too. The man was sure to hover at his elbow all night, ingratiating himself with Rupert's acquaintances and annoying his father, the Duke of Staines. Sanderson needed to get a life of his own instead of following Rupert around like a devoted puppy.

He stood before the mirror again, straightening his coat sleeves. A smiling gentleman stared back at him.

Am I truly as happy as I seem in this reflection?

He doubted it very much. He was restless, bored with his life. Rupert's heart no longer raced with excitement at the thought of seeing other people. Only Charles made him happy, and those moments were also filled with regret. That's what became of a man who'd lost his way as thoroughly as he had.

He's also a man who talks to himself a lot more than he needs to.

He pulled a face and then strolled for the door to his suite of rooms. Outside, Sanderson would be waiting— a man who expressed a wish to jolly him along. To be his brother and an uncle to Charlie. He was determined to present a united family front despite Sally's many indiscretions.

Smith approached in a rush. "His Grace has just sent word that he's had a change of heart about the Dunhill event and wanted to warn you he wouldn't be attending after all."

Bloody coward! Rupert bit back an oath. The last thing he wanted to do was stand about with Sanderson and people who all had wives at the same event. There would be whispers, questions about where Sally was tonight, as if he should know, and subtle hints about whose bed she might be warming. He did not want to see her flirt with other men.

He had no idea or wish to learn what she did. They say a man comes to understand the value of what he's lost by the end of his life. Rupert was a long way from the grave, but he was already aware he'd made a mistake he could never recover from.

Never let them see your pain.

He forced a smile, and sent Smith on his way with his thanks.

Sanderson waited for him at the base of the stairs appearing merry, dressed to stand out in another garish blue suit of clothes that rivaled his father's often poor tastes in fashion.

"I feared you'd become lost in your own house, Bracknell," Sanderson teased.

"I told you eight o'clock—" the clocks in the house chimed loudly, "—and so it now is."

Sanderson tugged on dark gloves. "I hear the duke is otherwise engaged tonight, so I wonder if I can persuade you to change our evening plans. Sally might not miss us so we could enjoy an hour or so of diverting amusements and revels before we go to the Dunhill Soiree?"

Ah, yes. Revels. Sanderson likely wished to visit a brothel. He was always trying to drag Rupert to low places where pleasure could be had for a price to make up for the fact Sally preferred everyone else. So far, Sanderson had no idea Rupert managed the scandalous Hunt Club, and he was very glad for his ignorance right now. The man was a reckless, pleasure-seeking fool. Sanderson would probably exhaust himself in whores' arms one day if he did not learn the value of moderation soon. Rupert just hoped he wasn't expected to indulge too. "What did you have in mind?"

"You know how I love to gamble, and you always enjoy more physical pursuits. There is a new establishment I have heard of that caters to both our needs. Everyone is whispering about the fights. It is said to be quite exciting. No rules at all."

"Boxing? At a hell or something?"

"No, no, no. Behind the hell. It is all very secluded

and discreet. Trust me, no one will know we attend."

It still sounded suspiciously like trouble. "Unless the watch is called."

"That almost never happens." Sanderson grinned. "You'll never be recognized if that's your concern. We'll only stay long enough to satisfy my curiously before heading to the Dunhill thing to meet Sally there. A half-hour diversion at most, I promise."

Rupert shook his head. "I do not worry about being recognized, and your sister would not care what I did."

Sally would probably prefer not to have her husband hovering about, spoiling her enjoyment of the evening.

Sanderson had always been sympathetic about the poor state of his marriage, and nodded solicitously. "This is just what you need. The risk is worth it for the adventure of trying something new. The Dunhill Soiree is bound to be a bore anyway until later. Anyway, I am going to venture to the hell whether you join me or not."

Sanderson strode out the door purposefully, leaving Rupert behind in the entrance hall looking at the high shine on his boots. The man was usually willing to rub elbows with the cream of society, but his love of gambling would surely get his throat cut in any low place like this one sounded.

Rupert saw no choice but to follow to keep the idiot out of harm's way.

CHAPTER THREE

Regrets afforded a man no comfort. Angelo certainly harbored a few too many to believe his death was to be anything but torture.

But it wouldn't be tonight.

The blind alley behind Wiggan's Boarding House stank of spilled ale, old blood and the stench of dozens of unwashed bodies. Angelo lifted a scrap of cloth to his nose, inhaling the sweet scent of cloves he'd sewn into a corner to overcome the urge to cast up his accounts there and then. Dear God, he missed Mayfair and the delicate cacophony of conflicting perfumes worn by the *ton*. "I'm ready," he assured his burly companions.

"Good. Now remember, don't end it too quick or the pot will be short," Wiggan cautioned, "I told Kirkland that his man should not strike your face, but he's a big one and dim with it."

"If he breaks my nose, I'll rip his balls off," Angelo warned, but drew himself up to his full height—a mere five foot six inches of lean muscle—ready for the fight to come.

"Now. Now. Now. Don't take a set against the poor sod too soon," Wiggan warned. "You needn't scare the pants off him straight away."

"That certainly wouldn't do," he chuckled. Angelo might appear a weakling compared to his usual array of opponents, but he was deceptively stronger and faster than anyone he'd faced in these fights so far. He'd had years of battle against more skilled opponents than those Kirkland and Wiggan could find. He'd fought against men who'd had no hesitation to make an attempt to end his life, nor had he hesitated to take theirs when it became inevitable. That he lived was proof of his prowess, rather than luck.

However, appearances mattered tonight, so he would curb his violent tendencies and avoid a life-threatening injury to his opponent. He was done with killing, or so he always hoped.

He eased away from the wall, studying the restless crowd ahead. The pickpockets were already at work, dipping their fingers into unguarded pockets. "As long as this latest fool performs the way we practiced the money will flow into your hands, and then into mine."

Wiggan rubbed his hands briskly in anticipation. "Kirkland promised there was a pair of puffed-up cits in the hell tonight. One's a wet goose that let slip the other's full of juice. With luck, they'll leave with pockets to let."

Angelo didn't particularly care who the victims of this little farce would be. Fleecing the rich was what Wiggan and Kirkland paid him well to make possible. He was the entertainment. The distraction while pockets were picked, outrageous wagers made and lost, and lives ruined.

If there had been a few foolish men to lose their lives after the melee was over, it was none of his damn business. He was never involved in anything beyond the main event, and he planned to always keep it that way.

Angelo followed two paces behind Wiggan to reach the spot where the crowd had gathered. Patrons of the Wiggan boarding house and also Kirkland's gambling establishment met on each side of the alley, each screaming out wagers for their fighter of choice.

Odds were always against him in the beginning. Even the ones in on the action dismissed his chances in a false display of pure cunning. They wanted him to win. They knew he would in the end.

The mood was high, the crowd loud as he drew closer slowly. Wagers were placed—not on who would win but on how long he'd remain on his feet, on how many strikes could connect to a body before he fell, grasping for an end to the bout.

These were not rules gentlemen fought by, but no one cared for the niceties of honor or dignity in the Seven Dials.

He paced to the center of the makeshift ring cleared by the crowd and, ready to begin, he flexed his shoulders to loosen up. He could perform tonight's routine in his sleep; however, his opponents sometimes forgot that he was always destined to win, so he did make an effort to prepare his body for action. The fellows he was pitted against sometimes got a little too enthusiastic about the show and had to be reminded, forcibly, not to really try to hurt him.

They touched his face at their own peril. He'd broken more than a few noses, and once an arm to halt a particularly engaged and enraged opponent from continuing the bout.

The crowd groaned as one and he turned to see a hulking giant of a man striding out of Kirkland's hell to meet him. The fellow smiled at Angelo with all the intelligence of a simpleton gleaming in his eyes. The crowd from Kirkland's chanted his name.

Willem. Willem.

The idiot beamed at his supporters as if it was his birthday and not a day he could die. Dear God, which bloody country paddock had they dredged this pathetic, brainless creature from? This was going to be painful. For both of them. Angelo preferred to hit someone who was aware that they put their life in jeopardy when they faced him.

Wiggan blathered on about the so-called rules, and at the prearranged spot in his little speech, the lard-bellied giant lurched forward and made an attempt to grab Angelo by the throat.

He dodged quickly and jabbed his fist into the fellow's thick side, almost bouncing off again. Willem was quick to catch up with him and spun about almost gracefully, striking out with a glancing blow to Angelo's shoulder.

Taken off guard by Willem's reach, Angelo stumbled sideways into the crowd and was shoved roughly back toward his adversary.

The fellow was ready. Had he been bullied about before this fight?

Good. At least he wouldn't stand still and take the beating as a previous fighter had done.

Willem swung for Angelo's head next, and he dodged back, keeping his face protected by raising one arm, and scowled. "Not the face, you bastard," he warned in a low growl.

Willem shrugged and swung again.

Angelo crouched low to avoid the meaty fist and jabbed into the big man's other soft side. Willem grunted, but Angelo held back the worst of his strength from the blow. The plan was to draw out the bout for at least twenty minutes, allowing all pockets to be picked and wagers placed first, not end the bout within the first five because he grew angry with his opponent.

They parried some more minutes, dancing and dodging as if they were evenly matched—Willem's strength and reach against Angelo's speed and precision.

It was almost too easy.

His attention flickered to the crowd and held there a fraction to long on a face so perfect and familiar, his breath caught.

The distraction allowed Willem to connect with Angelo's jaw. His head snapped back and he staggered to keep his balance. Beyond the shock of the blow, his heart squeezed in pain. Not from the fight, but from recognition.

He tasted blood and a red haze filled his vision. He shook off the pain and plowed into Willem, knocking him to the ground in his fury.

Lord Bracknell was in the crowd, and the saintly prig saw his real face and didn't even recognize him.

CHAPTER FOUR

Gods, what an unholy brawl.

Rupert clung to the weathered banister that led to the heights of a dilapidated boarding house, watching the fight despite his original intention of leaving. The mood of the crowd was wild. His ears rung as taunts for the Spaniard's downfall grew loud and extremely blunt. Clearly they all knew of him but the fellow took their scorn with good humor, bowing extravagantly and grinning despite his bleeding lip.

Perched higher than the crowd, Rupert's view of the fighters was clear. Perfect.

The Spaniard should stand no chance against the much larger man.

He'd be beaten to a bloody pulp, and then Rupert would find out where Sanderson had disappeared to. Most likely with the whore who'd been balanced on his lap the last time he'd seen the man.

"Bets. Bets." A fellow stopped at the base of the stairs and scowled at him. "This ain't a spectator sport, gov."

Keep your coin hidden.

Rupert negligently threw down a handful of coppers he had in his hand already. "On the giant to flatten the Spaniard in the next minute."

He eyed the pair again as they circled each other and then commenced trading blows. He'd win handily and call his evening a success. The smaller man was fast, agile, but strangely slow at other times.

Rupert watched eagerly as the fellow scaled the giant's back, caught him about the throat as if about to choke him. The man was cunning. Yet, for all that effort, he let the giant go and was tossed into the crowd.

It made no sense...and then it did.

Never let anyone see your true colors at first in a fight.

Always hold something back.

Only slow when it suited him, to lead the larger man into a careless charge. The minute passed and Rupert lost his money. He regarded the Spaniard with admiration. He was a superb actor.

"You lose," the fellow below said with a smug grin.

Rupert cursed and studied the crowd, noting a pocket getting picked out of the corner of his eye.

The bout wasn't a fair one—only a distraction from the real aim of the melee. The giant kept nodding too, and looking toward the hell's owner. Rupert cursed again that he'd listened to the crowds call for the Spaniard's blood before considering the matter properly. In a low place like this, half of the regulars had to be in on the scheme to fleece the unwary.

"Wait," he called, holding out a further coin he'd hidden in his other hand. "All on the Spaniard, and to win."

The fellow's eyes lit with greed. "Oh, ho. We are against each other. Care to make a further wager on the Spaniard?"

"No need."

Never give up more than you are prepared to lose forever.

"Why not?" he asked, eyeing him with more interest than Rupert cared for. "You've clearly got blunt enough to do as you wish."

"That's the last of it," he promised with a beleaguered sigh he hoped sounded convincing.

It was dangerous to have his situation as a man of means known in a place like this. In the wrong ears, that knowledge might see him fleeced or even beaten for his clothes and boots.

The fellow moved away and soon had his head together with a rough-looking man. A chill swept him as the pair snuck glances at him.

Fuck.

Rupert glanced around discreetly, fighting to keep his concern from his face.

Always know how to leave anyplace quickly, Angelo Marinari had warned him once.

He'd come to the alley via the hell's rear door,

looking for Sanderson among the crowd. Others had arrived via the boarding house behind him. There were dozens of rough-looking men between him and both doorways now. His skin pricked a warning that this could end badly if he was not careful.

The cleanest way out should be through this alley at either end.

A shout went up and he turned back to the fight as the Spaniard took a hard blow to his ribs and staggered.

Since everyone fell silent, Rupert heard the Spaniard's voice as he savagely cursed his opponent. "Lover of a whore's son. You'll pay for that, you ox."

A ripple of fear filled Rupert at the tone. Not for himself, but for the Spaniard's larger opponent. The Spaniard stripped off his shirt, raging, stalking around his opponent as if he could tear him limb from limb with his bare hands.

Rupert's breath caught and he couldn't seem to catch it again. The Spaniard was utterly magnificent in his rage. All lean muscle that rippled with each movement. Olive skin that glowed with sweat but appeared soft as butter, but bore the marks of nearly a dozen old wounds.

Rupert moved down into the crowd, drawn in for a closer look at the magnificent fighter.

Unfortunately, the Spaniard was dancing backward by then. The crowd parted, leading the fight directly toward Rupert.

He couldn't avoid the collision and flailed under the fighter's small weight for a few embarrassing moments. The Spaniard's eyes caught his briefly and Rupert groaned. The Spaniard stiffened away. He flipped back up to his feet, executing a move both fluid and practiced as he turned on his opponent with cruel blows.

The fight shifted away, as did the crowd, leaving Rupert to find his own feet at a far slower pace. He could still feel the Spaniard's small body, hot and vital, against his chest. It had felt...strangely good.

He flicked the filth from his coat and trousers and followed after the fight. He couldn't arrive at the ball now in soiled clothing, so he would stay to the end and then go home and change, with or without Sanderson.

A shiver raced over his skin and he looked around. Two ugly-looking fellows were watching him with cold, calculating eyes. Another man peeled off a nearby wall just as a loud cheer went up and the crowd moved into the hell.

He was vaguely aware that the Spaniard had indeed won the bout but he'd more on his mind than trying to collect his winnings.

He moved to follow everyone into the hell, but a large man blocked his way. "Lets have a little chat."

Cut off from the obvious escape route, Rupert turned and raced down the alley, only to discover it ended in a brick wall. There was no way out—and he'd been followed.

"We'll have the rest of your money now," a man said with a sneer. "And your fancy boots too."

Three against one.

Marinari's whispers of advice filled his memory. *If there's no chance of escape, fight is the only recourse. Make them pay for their insolence. Never let them see your fear.*

Rupert raised his fists; well aware he was outnumbered and outflanked. Seized by utter recklessness, he smiled at their leader. "Let's get this over with, shall we?"

CHAPTER FIVE

The dull ache of a dozen or more blows thundered through Angelo. By morning, he'd be black and blue all over. An ugly sight indeed. He dabbed at the cut on his lip, wincing inwardly at how rough he must look.

"Your share," Kirkland said as he tossed a pouch of coin across the strong room to him and another larger one to Wiggan. "There's a bonus for the split lip in there, Spaniard."

Angelo hefted the coins, judged them about right for their agreement, and then slipped it inside his shirt. He didn't bother to count his money now. Faith was a short-lived condition, and for now he chose to believe he'd not been swindled with his share. "My thanks," he mumbled around the discomfort of his cut lip.

He'd much rather the flow of his native tongue, but these idiots wouldn't understand him if he did. So he spoke Spanish accented English and pretended to stumble over certain words.

Wiggan rubbed his jaw. "I'll let you know about Sunday. Might be fighting elsewhere next time."

"Did the Cheapside Inn proprietor improve his offer?"

"Somewhat?" Kirkland muttered. It was hard to miss that the details of their bargaining lacked any sort of specific value to Angelo. "He's a bit worried about the establishment finding out our game."

"Announce the bout at the last moment," Angelo suggested, although anyone with sense would know that these fights were best conducted in near secrecy until the last moment.

The problem with that strategy though was the difficulty in attracting a large enough crowd to steal from.

"We'll need a swell to fleece. A few would be better."

Angelo's stomach lurched, remembering Bracknell's

face in the crowd. He hadn't seen him after the bout and hoped the man was all right. He cursed himself roundly for caring. "I thought you had a pair tonight?"

"One emptied his pockets quick smart once he understood he'd have no choice and fled."

Ah, good. Bracknell had acted sensibly. As much as he'd disliked seeing Bracknell again, he was glad to know he'd wisdom enough to know when to leave. There was no mercy for the well-to-do when they strayed into this territory.

Angelo discreetly held his ribs as the ache there intensified. He'd have to bind them tonight. But would he be well enough for another bout by Sunday? *Perhaps.* He drew in a deep breath and winced at the pain of his ribs. *Perhaps not.* His opponent tonight had not been acting for much of the fight. There had been brute strength behind every one of Willem's punches. Most likely Angelo was damaged enough to need the luxury of bed rest for a few days.

He said nothing of his injuries however. Nothing of his concerns for the upcoming fight. Wiggan cared for nothing but the money Angelo made him. Besides, Kirkland would attempt to take advantage if he sensed weakness. He'd try to retrieve his fee, and Angelo could not spare the funds.

He bid his partners in crime adieu then strolled out into the alley to return to the stairs that led to his attic room in the boarding house, senses still high from the fight and alert to any danger lurking in the shadows. It sometimes happened that a loser, wagering more than he could afford to lose, sought him out afterward to extract his revenge in private. He stepped lightly and did his best to avoid killing the poor sods.

After so long living alone, he could have no one here suspecting he'd excelled at murder.

His discretion had saved him as many times as his strength.

Although...it would have been nice to have some warning that Lord Bracknell had been standing in the crowd tonight. He'd stumbled in surprise at seeing him again after so long apart. Although enraged at first, he was glad Bracknell had not recognized him in male attire now.

He *was* supposed to be dead after all.

As he ran up the first flight, a man grunted to his left. Then again in pain.

Great pain.

Although it was unwise to become involved, Angelo was drawn back down the stairs to investigate the sounds. Another fool was about to lose his life. Usually the murderers waited until nearer to dawn to finish off their prey.

Their eagerness tonight intrigued him, and he was determined to discover the reason for such haste. He reached the end of the blind alley and stopped.

Three brutish men stood about a fourth who was on his knees, stretched out between two as he was beaten time and again. These were some of Kirkland's men and Angelo knew their tempers to be volatile at best, even worse when thwarted. He cast a pitying glance at the man on the ground. *Fool.* The high shine of his boots in the flickering moonlight and excellent cut of his seemingly drab coat gave him away as a member of the upper class.

They pulled the man's dark head back and then delivered another blow that should have killed the poor fellow. He spat blood instead and laughed.

The fellow was going to die, or come very close to it unless someone intervened.

Angelo took a silent step forward.

"Search him again," the leader demanded.

The fellow's coat was ripped off and then apart, every pocket checked, every seam tested for hidden coins in the lining. They threw the coat aside. "Nothing."

The remaining man patted down their victim's shirt. "Got something about his neck. Might be worth something."

He held up a string of beads high, and a glint of gold at the end caught Angelo's full attention.

"Give it back, you lover of a whore's son!" the man on the ground spat out.

The hair on the back of Angelo's neck stood on end.

In that moment, Angelo recognized Lord Bracknell.

There was no man alive more stubborn not to have given up already.

Cold rage filled him, unlike anything he'd ever felt before. Angelo curled his fingers into fists and boldly stepped forward just as Bracknell was dealt another blow that knocked him down.

Made him still and silent.

Angelo, little caring who the men worked for now, put them in their places.

He put them on the ground, unable to rise ever again.

The only sound that remained was the ragged breaths of the Earl of Bracknell.

Angelo searched the assailants' pockets, recovering several items that undoubtedly belonged to Bracknell, and then hurried to the earl's side after snatching up his coat.

Bracknell was insensible.

Angelo ran his hands over the earl's face carefully, felt his breath against his palm, and despite the pain of his ribs, hauled his dead weight upright, and then bent him over his shoulder. Angelo carried him, biting back an oath at the sharp, stinging pain of his ribs, and walked back the way he'd come, past the boarding house and the hell's back doors, through the twisted alley and into another, and another, until he deemed it safe to hail a hack.

The coachman, bundled up against the chill night air, regarded him warily, but as a coin flicked out toward him, he nodded. Angelo gave directions to a Golden Square address and eased the earl inside the dark carriage.

Once they were moving, Angelo skimmed his fingers over Bracknell's chest once more and pressed lightly over his heart. It beat steadily against his fingertips, and Angelo was relieved beyond words for that small reassurance.

Bracknell's head lolled to the side on the next corner and Angelo gently cradled his head against his shoulder so he could not be injured further. Dear God, he had loved this man once. Enough to walk away from the pain of rejection without bitterness, knowing it was his only choice.

"Wake up, beloved," he whispered to the man falling farther into his arms. "Wake up and see me as I really am."

Bracknell did not stir. He did not react in any way at all to Angelo's touch or tender words.

Something he'd never done before. They'd had moments, close encounters when emotions had run high, but it had always been Bracknell fighting the attraction and backing away. Now it would be Angelo's turn.

He had no regrets that he'd loved this man in vain all those years ago.

It simply wasn't meant to be.

He peered out the window, relieved to see the Duke of Staines' London residence not too far ahead. The upper front windows shone with light despite the late hour, which meant the duke was most definitely in residence for the season, and where the Duke of Staines went, his man Francis Redding was never far behind. Redding was a man who knew more about healing than many men in the profession.

Redding could be counted on.

Trusted without question.

He would tend to the duke's heir and decide when Bracknell was well enough to return to his wife and son.

Angelo had the carriage stop not far from the dwelling; he eased from beneath Bracknell's limp body and climbed out of the carriage. Damn, but his ribs hurt like the devil now, but there was no time to look after himself. He held up another coin to the driver, far more than the fare was worth, but kept his face hidden. "Drive on to the Duke of Staines' residence and deliver the other man to the door. I'll be watching what happens next, so you'd better be quick smart about it."

The coachman swallowed nervously, glancing down at the silent carriage. He must be wondering if Bracknell were dead in there.

"Take him and hurry," Angelo demanded. "His life depends upon it."

"Right you are, sir," the coachman said as he

slapped the reins, rolling onto Tindel House's impressive portico. He scurried up the stairs, pounded long and hard on the door until it was flung open. Angelo shifted into the shadows of a home across the street for a better view of the encounter and watched, heart pounding a little. It did not take long for servants to swarm out and Bracknell's still body to be carried inside by three footmen.

Angelo hunkered down on a cold stair, waiting to see if the coachman would reveal the direction he'd taken. The coachman was escorted inside for questioning, his carriage held before the house and searched. He caught a glimpse of Redding's shocked face as he glanced up and down the street before he expelled a breath of frustration.

Longing for what he'd never had—people who cared about him—wasn't wise.

The duke's door slammed shut as Angelo began to shiver.

He could go now, return home to rest his weary body. And yet he was curious why one of the wealthiest men in London had frequented the most dangerous hell in the city. Bracknell attended Gentleman Jackson's boxing establishment, for pity's sake, not to mention he had the decadent Hunt Club where any pleasure could be indulged in absolute privacy—including private bouts.

Had he learned nothing from Angelo's past warnings?

CHAPTER SIX

"Where am I?" Rupert asked thickly, puzzled by the unfamiliar sounds and voices around him.

"Oh, thank heavens," his father exclaimed loud enough to make him wince. He felt hands slide over his arm and grasp his hand tightly. Rupert cursed as pain shot up his arm and his father quickly releasing him. "You gave us one hell of a scare, son," Father said.

When he tried to open both eyes, he discovered he could not do it. Rupert looked about with one eye, recognizing he was in a dimly lit bedchamber but not much else was familiar. There was a strong scent of herbs in the room, and his chest was warm and heavy as if something lay upon it. He turned his head slowly, as it thumped with pain, and discovered Francis Redding frowning down upon him too.

"What are you doing hovering over my bed, Red?"

The man's expression flickered across the room and back. "You're at Tindel House, in my bedchamber, my lord."

That was ridiculous. He'd no cause to be here. He must be drunk. He must be delirious or having a nightmare. He struggled to clear his mind as Redding lifted the weight from his chest and set it aside. "I am..."

He faltered. His mind was utterly blank of anything before he had opened his one good eye. He gripped the sheet, or tried to, but found his hands were useless, bandaged thickly and sore as hell.

"Try not to move," Redding warned. "You've taken one hell of a beating. You're lucky to be alive. What happened to you?"

He closed his good eye, trying hard to remember. When he licked his lips, they hurt too, and he discovered his lip had been split open. "I remember..." He swallowed at the panic that filled him at remembering. "Being on my knees. I was held. Outnumbered."

"Go on." His father eased onto the bed and rested one hand gently on his chest.

It hurt a little to breathe with it there, so he pushed aside his father with the back of his bandaged hand.

He struggled to recall more. Images shifted. Fear. Pain. And eventually safety. "A dark carriage."

"Hmm, a hack brought you home, but you were alone in it by the time it drew up before the house. Can you remember anything before you got into the carriage?"

"I don't remember getting in." A memory suddenly snapped into focus. "Sanderson."

"What about him?"

"We were at a hell together. I lost sight of him at Kirkland's gambling establishment." Rupert struggled to sit up and both Redding and father had to help him, stuffing a mountain of pillows behind his back and arms. "I feel terrible," he complained.

Father ruffled his hair carefully. "As always, the master of understatement, son."

Redding chuckled as he fiddled with a tray beside the bed. He returned to sit beside him with a bowl and spoon in hand. Rupert focused on him in horror. "Is Sanderson all right? Did he make it out alive?"

"He is fine and at your home as far as I know." Father moved to the door and gave a servant standing outside an order he couldn't quite hear. He returned quickly and stood behind Redding, hands on the man's broad shoulders.

Redding brought the spoon to Rupert's mouth. "Sip this, my lord."

Rupert regarded Redding and the spoon warily. "What is in it?"

His father laughed. "He still doesn't trust your concoctions, my friend."

"Nothing to harm you," Redding promised. "Have a little now, and then we will talk."

For a change, Rupert went along with it. He was hungry, now he was awake.

He managed seven sips before Redding set aside the

bowl and spoon. "Who did this to you?"

"I don't know," he said, realizing the broth had left behind a subtle aftertaste. He scowled at Redding, fuming silently that he'd been cleverly tricked. Redding merely smiled, a slight twist of his lips, but his concern remained. Rupert glanced away from him. "I didn't recall seeing the ruffians before. They were after money and such. They took everything I had on me."

Keep the rosary safe for me. It's all I have left of them.

Rupert fumbled at his chest, searching frantically beneath his shirt for the hidden keepsake with his bandaged hands. His neck was bare of it now, and he cursed. The last and only memento of that mad bastard was gone.

"Calm yourself, my lord," Redding cautioned. He placed a gentle hand on Rupert's brow, testing him for fever. Then he checked his wrist, feeling for the pulse. He nodded. "There's nothing you need do now but rest."

He had to get the piece back. He tried to rise but Redding barred his way gently. "You'll only hurt yourself more if you continue to struggle. The duke has sent out men to investigate the matter. I promise we will leave no stone unturned to discover who did this to you."

Rupert sank back, struggling to hold in a groan of pain and failing. He gasped for breath as the pain became unbearable. By the time he was recovered, his head was swimming in new images. "They would have killed me."

"You have a hard head and stubborn disposition," Redding murmured, but his father's breath caught and he rushed out of the room suddenly, dark coat flapping behind him.

Rupert squinted at the far door. "What's wrong with him?"

"Forgive him. He's been at your bedside since the moment you arrived and would barely agree to leave you for even five minutes," Redding explained as he fumbled about with a bowl of water and cloth on a side table. He placed the cold, sodden rag on Rupert's forehead and sat back with a nod. "He's quite overset but he'll calm down, now that you're finally awake."

"Finally?"

"You've been insensible for two days," Redding murmured softly.

Rupert peered around the room, struggling to accept the lost days, and noticed that it was dark outside now. "What time is it?"

"Eleven in the evening." Redding sighed. "A lot has happened, my lord. But first, can you remember who put you in the carriage?"

Rupert shook his head and instantly regretted the gesture. His senses swam and he grabbed at Redding to steady himself. "I don't know. I don't remember anything but the men who stole from me."

Redding's lips puckered as he considered Rupert. "You still have your usual valuables. Money, signet ring." He dug in his pocket. "These were found in the pocket of your coat that had been nearly sliced to pieces. You even have this."

Redding swung Marinari's rosary before Rupert's eyes.

Rupert snatched it back, hiding it beneath the sheets guiltily. He'd never told anyone he'd kept a piece of Angelo Marinari with him at all times.

"I know who once owned something like that." Redding sighed heavily and retrieved it. He slipped it over Rupert's head and hid it beneath his nightshirt. "It seems to me you might have a guardian *angel* watching over you. You were brought to Tindel House directly rather than your own home. Only someone who knew us would do that. It took some time, but the coachman was persuaded to reveal that a fierce-looking man put you in the carriage. He said he was not threatened, but felt it just the same."

See me as I really am someone had whispered. Rupert struggled to hold on to the memory of that deep male voice, but it slipped away too quickly, thanks to Redding's medicinal broth. He tried to focus on Redding's face but began to have trouble keeping his eyes open.

"Tell me, you didn't seek to fight after you heard about her?"

Rupert struggled to focus. "What *her* are you talking about?"

"Lady Bracknell. Sally." Redding raked his fingers through his hair. "Did you go to the hell after you heard about your wife?"

A dark shape slipped into the room, and Rupert couldn't keep his eyes open anymore but he thought his father had returned. "Where is Sally?"

It would have been very considerate and kind if his wife had come to sit by his sickbed. She had such gentle hands.

"She's dead, Ru," his father whispered. "They found her at the bottom of a staircase at the Dunhill Soiree. Her neck was broken, some say from a fall."

Despite his creeping tiredness, pain flared through Rupert's heart at the news. Redding's potion was hard to fight but he tried anyway. "Some?"

"She would never use the servants' stairs in the Dunhill home and because of that, there are whispers going around suggesting she was murdered. Did you see her that night?"

"Never made it to Dunhill's," he promised through lips grown thick and uncooperative. He wet them. "She was the one who pushed me away long ago," he whispered before oblivion claimed him.

CHAPTER SEVEN

Perhaps his favorite fruit was peach.

Angelo sliced away the skin carefully and bit into soft flesh, allowing the juices to dribble down his chin unheeded.

He was in a bit of a mood today. Restless again, and angry. His body sore from the fight and from lugging Lord Bracknell about over his shoulder.

His dissatisfaction was not entirely with his own slow recovery, however, but with the world at large. It was clear that nothing about London would ever change. The gentry were so very foolish but not usually stupid. He'd made the mistake of reading a recent newssheet, received the news of Lady Bracknell's tragic fall, and had been stunned by the blatant suspicion leveled at her husband.

That sort of nonsense was ludicrous, given the extent of Bracknell's injuries. Imagine claiming the earl had murdered his wife the same night Angelo had rescued him from his own certain death. They said Bracknell had fled to the duke's home to beg his protection. Only a coward murdered women and Lord Bracknell was most definitely not one of those.

He finished his peach and flicked the pit out the window, watching it roll away across the adjoining roof to mingle with other refuse.

It simply wasn't possible for a man to be in two places at one time.

He glared at his narrow bed, at the corner of newssheet just visible under the straw mattress, where he'd stuffed it in disgust. The report bothered him for what it did not say about the evening. Bracknell had been alone at the fight, so of course his whereabouts could not be proven.

Not unless Angelo came forward to clear his name.

It annoyed him more than he thought possible that

he, a dead man, might be needed as a witness to prevent Bracknell from being interrogated.

He shook his head to banish a surge of anger at that image, and exited the tiny attic room, seeking a solid meal to appeal his growing hunger and men of his own level in the common room below. The men in the taproom would not care for the ill fortune of others and put self-preservation first, forever and always.

He belonged here.

He felt it in his bones.

The common room was quiet, only a handful of drunks sitting in gloomy corners nursing tankards at this early hour. There was a man alone with his large-brimmed hat placed over his knee in the far corner, and another draining the last of his ale opposite.

He slid into a chair at an unoccupied table close to an easy exit and flicked a coin to the cook when he finally appeared. "Ale and stew if you have any."

The fellow grunted sourly, but went to fetch Angelo's requests.

On his return, he slid the bowl at him roughly. "Did anyone tell you what happened in the alley after the last fight?"

"No." What happened after the fight was none of his business. There had been at least twenty murders in the lane behind the boarding house since he'd taken a room six months ago. Angelo had kept his mouth shut about each and every one. There was nothing to say and no evidence had ever been left behind. Bodies were always taken away to befoul someone else's neighborhood or were thrown in the great river.

He groaned under his breath, realizing he'd made a careless mistake. In his haste to protect Bracknell, he'd failed to clean up his mess upon his return. He'd gone to bed to nurse his injuries and supped on his store of fruit until forced to remerge today. He did not think it likely, but one of the men who'd attacked Bracknell might have clung to life, and be able to identify him.

"Kirkland lost three good men after the fight," cook continued at a whisper, his gaze darting around the room. "They were left in the lane as a warning. One of Kirkland's rivals is making a move on his territory."

"Why do you say that?" he asked, knowing some response was required. Battles for territory were a regular occurrence around here.

Angelo calmed and sipped his ale. He was in luck. He'd killed those men and could not be identified. He felt no regret. He never had in all the years he'd been an assassin.

"It's obvious," the cook said as he eased closer. "Your room up there has a view of the lane. Did you see nothing at all?"

"I wasn't around." He shoveled food in his mouth as he worked on concocting a plausible lie. "Took a stroll after the fight and had a wench under me until the sun rose."

Cook chuckled dryly. "Which lucky lass caught your eye?"

Angelo grinned wickedly. There had been no woman, of course, and there never would be. He preferred strength and hard flesh against him for pleasure, not the soft curves of a woman. "Never you mind. She's mine."

Cook drew back, apparently satisfied with his story, and went off to serve another customer when called.

Angelo finished his meal at a leisurely pace, but in the background, he could hear the talk about his handiwork. The speculation got his blood pumping again. He remembered passing no one on his way to the Duke of Staines' residence, but that did not mean he hadn't gone entirely unnoticed. He couldn't be certain now that, given his injuries, he had been entirely silent as he'd carried Bracknell to safety. He reached for his hat and nodded a farewell to cook.

The man jerked his head. "Where are you off to now?"

Cook had never questioned him before, and Angelo's skin pricked with alarm. "Out and about."

Cook nodded. "Watch your back?"

Angelo frowned. "For what?"

"For anyone that doesn't belong in these parts," he warned. "You work for Kirkland and he's taking this seriously, and so should everyone."

Bloody hell! The killer, *he*, was being hunted.

Angelo knew better than to react—to make a dash out to the street or even move swiftly before he was at least three streets away. If he were being followed about, Angelo would have to be cautious yet remain above suspicion for some time. Not that he had any plans to move on just yet. The first rule in hiding your crimes was to never flee the scene.

So he swaggered out the door, turned southeast for the crossroads, and then sauntered more southerly to visit Covent Garden. While there, he purchased an orange, peeled and ate it as he zigzagged through the streets of Holborn. He noted the man in the overlarge hat from the common room had followed him. The fellow wasn't very good at blending in really, and Angelo hid a smile. *Amateurs!*

Making a show of being at a loose end and carefree, he entered a tavern he knew well just as a brawl ended.

Perfect timing. He sipped a pint of well-watered ale while the blood on the floor was washed away, and then wagered half his winnings from the fight on a game of hazard. He allowed his hard-earned money to be lost while keeping a watchful eye on everyone. The man following him had changed his hat and coat, and gambled now across the room but far more cautiously than Angelo did. He clutched his single pint of ale too and only sipped infrequently.

Following a mark was always dull work and the man was easy to confuse when the patrons returned for the evening. Once Angelo had gambled all he could spare, he paid for a whiskey he didn't drink, watched others bet and lose, and disappeared from the follower's line of sight the moment his back was turned. To the casual observer, he would look like he was slipping out to take a piss, as any man might be expected to do, but he slipped through the back gate and into the mews.

Confident he'd acted as if nothing were wrong, he strolled along boldly now. He even whistled.

Angelo hailed a hack travelling west on Great Russell Street, quickly deciding it would be best to visit a better part of London for a while. It was a place many went during the day but few belonged late at night. It was a place hardly favored by the men he boxed for.

He went to Bond Street.

He strolled up and down the street, peering into dark shop fronts and passing a pleasant few hours deciding what he liked best in the window displays. He also admired a few men who passed him too, received an inviting smile from one fellow who he chose not to encourage. He wasn't one for picking up unknown gents to play with in the dark anymore.

He'd learned to be cautious with his affections.

He went to visit a spinster who secretly rented out her brother's attic room to gents who promised to be very, very quiet. He paid the modest fee, and rested under an old comforter by an attic window as night passed into new day while he pondered his next steps.

He could not get out of his mind that the man he foolishly still loved was under a cloud of suspicion. If Bracknell remained that way, he'd most likely be taken in by the authorities and questioned. Angelo knew too well the ways confessions could be coerced.

Angelo couldn't have that, but nor could he come forward himself as a witness to clear the earl's name. He was dead to the world and had murdered three men recently, and many more besides in past years on orders. He would be the worst sort of support for the earl.

He dozed until daybreak. Fresh of mind on waking, he stood and stretched, deciding that there might be a way to help Bracknell if he could find someone to claim to have been with Bracknell that night and save him from suspicion. But who?

There was but one man he trusted in London, though Redding couldn't be in two places at once—saving Bracknell at the hell and receiving him wounded at the duke's residence wasn't possible. Angelo had to find someone else. Someone with no morals or scruples about telling a fib or two.

He needed… Angelo clicked his fingers. He needed the man who'd killed him.

He needed Lord Beecroft's assistance.

Angelo knew his usual haunts. There were three locations Beecroft could be at this time of year.

He could be at his London townhouse, where there

were always a great many staff lurking about, half of them armed at all times.

He could be at the Hunt Club later in the afternoon—somewhere Angelo preferred not to return to under any circumstances.

Angelo peered further along the street. Hawke, Knight and Mumford Bank opened in an hour's time. The earl had taken an interest in finance and investment years ago to disguise he was courting the bookish proprietor of the establishment. He thought the pair were still together, although they probably lived apart much of the time.

When not at home, Beecroft could be at his lover's private residence a few streets away from the bank.

The residence made a more discreet setting for the kind of discussion he wanted to have with the man who'd shot him. He settled back under the blanket.

Angelo hid in the attic room until midday and then snuck out to the street. He strolled toward the bank and arrived just as the place was closing for luncheon. Mr. Victor Knight stepped out, alone and seemingly in something of a rush.

Angelo followed Mr. Knight all the way to his apartment door, but the man never looked back once to see if he was being followed. *Fool.* Hadn't Beecroft taught him anything about self-preservation?

It was easy to grab Victor Knight by the throat at his door, force him inside his home and tie him to a dining room chair before he could cry out.

Hardly out of breath, Angelo seated himself opposite and smiled. "Scream for help if you want your lover to die."

The man squinted. In the struggle, Knight's wire-rimmed glasses had been knocked to the ground. Angelo fetched them and returned them to the banker's face.

Victor Knight met his gaze. "I don't have any money here."

He shrugged. "If I wanted money, I'd steal it."

"Then what do you want?"

"Information. Where is Lord Beecroft right now?"

Knight's eyes darted toward the doorway,

unconsciously giving away that the earl was expected to arrive soon. No wonder the man seemed in a hurry. He must be here for a midday tryst with his lover.

Angelo smirked. "Good."

Knight paled. "Don't hurt him. I'll give you anything you want."

"A plea for Beecroft's life? My, my, is it love after all?" Unexpected envy filled Angelo. He'd never had that himself. "As long as Beecroft can be agreeable, you have nothing to fear from me."

Knight gulped. "And if he isn't?"

"Best pray that he loves you well." He gagged the man with his neckcloth and started to poke around the place. He'd just found a pistol, recognized it as his own, when his senses prickled a warning. He calmly loaded the weapon.

Victor Knight struggled when footsteps pounded up the staircase outside the apartment. Angelo took a seat and leveled the pistol directly at Victor Knight's head. "Be quiet now and let a dead man talk to his murderer."

No sooner were the words out of his mouth than Beecroft burst into the room, grinning widely. The smile dropped instantly, and so did the man's impressive shoulders when his eyes fell on Angelo. His muscles bunched again as he took in the situation. His instincts appeared as keen as ever, despite his years of retirement.

Unperturbed by this, Angelo merely smiled. "Hello, killer. Did you miss me?"

"Fuck," Beecroft cursed and shut the door with his foot. He stared long and hard at Angelo, and all the fighting tension drained away. "I thought I'd never see you again."

"Hoped, more likely." Angelo tapped the pistol against Knight's temple. "Stay right there. You're going to do exactly as I say or...you can probably guess what happens next."

Beecroft's eyes narrowed. "What do you want?"

Angelo told him, annoyed when the man only smiled after he'd made his request.

"He'll want to see you," Beecroft murmured softly.

"He never wanted to see me," Angelo grumbled then aimed the pistol at Knight's head again. He adjusted his aim for the slight misalignment of sight and barrel and knew he'd kill the banker with one shot. "Stick to the plan and hurry back. It's been days since I killed anyone. I'm growing bored, and my finger is tiring fast."

CHAPTER EIGHT

"I'm sorry. I cannot be entirely sure where Lord Bracknell went that night." Sanderson's expression turned grim as he spoke to the gentleman investigating Sally's murder on behalf of Bow Street. He gestured toward Rupert. "I left the hell well before any of this had happened to him."

Mr. William Forsythe had soaked up every word so far without comment and Rupert was feeling decidedly angry toward his brother-in-law. It was *his* idea to venture to that gambling establishment, after all. Couldn't he at least give him the benefit of the doubt?

Forsythe frowned. "Are you certain you didn't see his attackers?"

"As certain as I can be. I admit we were at the hell in Holborn earlier in the evening for a lark, but then Lord Bracknell excused himself, to use the privy I thought. I don't know where he disappeared to after that. He never returned to me, and I went on to the soiree alone. I didn't come upon Sally until I heard the screams." Sanderson turned his head aside and a sound suspiciously like a muffled sob could be heard. He turned back a few moments later, taking a deep breath before speaking. "Someone murdered my sister that night, and you must make them pay."

Rupert agreed. He was frustrated that he couldn't prove his innocence in the matter of Sally's death. He'd gone to the tavern with Sanderson, his mind was clear on that score, but after that his memory was a little murky at the edges still.

Forsythe frowned again. "Might I ask what was the nature of your conversation with him that night? Before the fight. Before Lord Bracknell claims he was attacked."

"I was attacked as you can plainly see."

"Nothing unusual, as far as I recall," Sanderson said

slowly. "We spoke of family, and—oh, as I said nothing out of the ordinary."

Sanderson quickly looked away, biting his lip.

The investigator pounced on his reticence. "What was it you were about to say?"

Sanderson stared at Rupert a long moment. "You spoke of Sally's defection again."

Rupert remembered some of that. Sanderson had surprised him by asking if he knew the identity of Sally's latest lover. Since he didn't, and they were in the middle of a crowded tavern, Rupert had not wished to discuss the matter, and certainly not with her brother. He'd been curt, to say the least.

"Defection? Were you estranged?"

"Many lords and their wives carry on with separate lives and interests after marriage," his father added quickly. "Its hardly unusual among the *ton*."

"We've not been close for some time," Rupert admitted as he shifted his bound arm.

He could tell by the way Forsythe glanced at his notes all the time that he was working up to an accusation that Rupert had somehow crossed London, killed his wife, and returned to the tavern to be beaten to within an inch of his life.

But to accuse a peer of murder was no small matter. He would need more than a lack of alibi before he proceeded with an outright accusation.

Rupert had no reason to wish for Sally's death. They may not have lived as man and wife in years, but that did not mean he had wished for his freedom that badly.

Forsyth sighed and shut his notebook. "Lord Bracknell, it would be appreciated if—"

The Tindel House butler barged in without knocking. "Your Grace, there is a caller you must speak with immediately."

Redding rose smoothly to head off the interruption. "His Grace is a little busy, Rigby."

Rigby struggled to see past Redding. "Yes, I know, but it is imperative His Grace speaks with Lord Beecroft *now*."

"Yes, all right, very well. Do show him in." Father didn't ask the investigator if the interruption suited him, and the poor man was wise enough not to protest.

Rupert took a moment to consider what more he could possibly do to prove his innocence. His word was all he had. None of the fellows at the tavern would recognize him, and if they did, it was unlikely they would alibi him without financial incentive to loosen their tongues.

Lord Beecroft rushed in, looking harried. He glanced about the room quickly and made a beeline for Rupert. "My condolences on the loss of your wife, man. How tragic you both faced death at almost the same moment."

Forsythe seized on his words. "What do you mean? At the same moment?"

"Ah, you must be Forsythe. A pleasure to finally meet you. Lord Beecroft, at your service. I believe we have a mutual connection in the Home Office. Lord sends his regards by the way, and asked that I assist in the investigation, since I was present when Lord Bracknell was attacked." Beecroft seated himself.

Forsythe blinked and glanced at Rupert swiftly. "Lord Beecroft was with you?"

"Indeed," Beecroft said with a firm nod before Rupert could deny it.

Rupert hadn't spoken to Lord Beecroft in months. They were not friends, nor ever likely to be.

Forsythe appeared a little wild about the eyes as Beecroft took command of the investigation with his next words. "Now what do we know are the facts of the matter in Lady Bracknell's murder?"

"Very little. Unfortunately the event was a crush and no one can remember if they saw Lord Bracknell there or not, although he had most definitely accepted the invitation," Forsythe admitted, fiddling with his notebook again. "There were no witnesses to Lady Bracknell's fall. I had hoped Lord Bracknell might shed further light on what might have happened to her."

"I would say he could not," Beecroft assured the investigator. "Tell me, what do you think the odds are that when Lord Bracknell was being beaten near to death, his wife was falling down those stairs to hers? Ghastly night all round, wouldn't you say?"

"Indeed," Father agreed. "Losing Sally is a tragedy.

The two events so near together bear investigation."

"And it shall be done, and thoroughly too." Beecroft peered into Rupert's face, and then sighed. "At least you can see through both eyes now. I thought you were done for, but I put you in the carriage and sent you off to Mr. Redding here because if anyone could set you to rights, it would be him. How are the ribs feeling today?"

Puzzled, Rupert brushed his hand over his side. Only Father and Redding and a few of the most loyal household staff would know the full extent of his injuries. "A little tender yet," he admitted cautiously.

"Well, rest as best you can. That boy of yours will need you more than ever now that his mother is gone." Beecroft drew close to Forsythe. "Now, have you got as far as compiling a list of possible suspects, Forsythe?"

"I am doing so at this very moment."

"Good, if I might have a word in private, sir." He glanced at Rupert with an apologetic wince. "Official business."

Transparently intrigued, Forsythe trotted across the chamber after Lord Beecroft.

Rupert took a steadying breath as they whispered in low tones. When Forsythe began to make very fast notes in his little book, nodding all the while, Rupert glanced at his brother-in-law. "Why did you leave me that night?"

"Forgive me, but it was you who abandoned me." Sanderson frowned and then called out to Lord Beecroft and Forsythe. "What are you saying about the night my sister died?"

"Nothing I can repeat at this moment, but," Beecroft shrugged, "this mostly has to do with the illegal fight Lord Bracknell stumbled upon behind Kirkland's. Bad business, that. I am lucky to have been on hand."

Father leaned forward. "Were you not invited to the Dunhill Soiree, Beecroft?"

"I sent my apologies a week ago. I do not care for dancing." He glanced down at Forsythe's little book and stabbed his finger to the page and continued talking to the investigator. "I met with Bracknell at Kirkland's, about nine o'clock I believe, and then we were lured into watching the fight in the alleyway behind. Damn shoddy business. Pickpockets and thieves. Those bastards would have ended my life too if I'd turned left instead of right."

Sanderson frowned and interrupted the pair again. "So you *saw* Lord Bracknell being beaten and did nothing?"

Beecroft shook his head sadly. "I did not see the attack itself. I was distracted and returned to find him unconscious on the cobblestones in inches of filth. I managed to run off his attackers though and dragged him to safety. After that, I sent him off in a hack and went directly to visit friends with the power to round up the ringleaders. Time was of the essence. Unfortunately, there was no one to catch that night, but we are getting close to identifying the perpetrators."

Forsythe tapped his pencil on his pad. "What time did you and Lord Bracknell part company?"

"I would have put Bracknell in the hack a little after eleven. Had the devil of a time finding one that would stop—me with a man slung over my shoulder. Can you imagine how that must have looked? I swear the coachman thought Bracknell was dead at first."

Rupert stared as Beecroft started to chuckle, remembering something he'd forgotten until now. "*You* carried me?"

Beecroft winced. "If you don't mind me saying, my lord, perhaps ease off the pork chops at dinner for a while. Almost broke my back lugging you about."

Rupert sat back, trying make his memory fit with Beecroft's story. The details Lord Beecroft mentioned were there in his mind now, but not the man himself. He and Beecroft were not close. He was a member of the Hunt Club though.

If in doubt, do not commit. Find a way to expose the motive later.

He chose his words carefully, wondering if he was being led into more trouble, and why Beecroft would do that to him. They'd not had much to do with each other for several years. Not since he'd shot Angelo and presumably killed him. "I thought the Spaniard was done for against that idiot brute they set him up against. My attention was on the fight until it was too late to escape their trap."

Beecroft winced again. "I am sorrier than you can imagine that we became separated. I had my pockets picked. Damn inconvenient. They stole my favorite pocket watch."

The investigator cleared his throat. "How long would you say Lord Bracknell was out of your sight?"

"No more than two or three minutes at most until he went into the carriage. It could have taken no more than twenty minutes for the hack to come here directly." He glanced at Bracknell. "I'm sorry I bothered chasing after them now. Can you forgive me?"

Rupert had not been in the tavern with Beecroft, but his words were the alibi he needed to prove his innocence in Sally's death. Beecroft's mention of time proved there had not been enough of it to travel from Dean Street to the Dunhill home to supposedly murder his wife unless he could suddenly fly the distance, which no man could ever do. He might be relieved to have this alibi, but he was also highly suspicious of Lord Beecroft's motives for giving it. "Of course."

The investigator stood. "I believe that will be all I need from you today, my lords. Your Grace. Please again accept my condolences for the loss of your dear lady."

Rupert stood and held out his good hand. "Thank you for coming to see me, sir. If there is any other news concerning the events surrounding my wife's death, you will find me at Bracknell House from this evening. I want to be kept informed of everything you discover from now on."

"Of course." The investigator bowed stiffly to the duke and left, his expression grim.

Sanderson glared at Beecroft sourly. "Why did you wait until today to come forward?"

"I've been caught up in the hunt for Bracknell's assailants, and I wanted to give him time to recover and to grieve before I showed my face again. Once I'd caught up on my correspondence and the gossip, I rushed right over."

"I see. What new leads did you mention?"

"I, ah..." Beecroft grimaced. "I thought to spare Bracknell the embarrassment of identifying the men

Lady Bracknell was currently involved with."

Sanderson recoiled, turning white with shock. "How dare you peddle gossip about Sally?"

"I only related what I had witnessed myself." Beecroft frowned at Sanderson. "I know it is difficult to hear, but Lords Deveraux, Peterson and Mr. Lovett must be considered in any proper investigation."

Rupert winced. Those men were Sanderson's close acquaintances too.

Sanderson tugged down his plum satin waistcoat, rightly furious. "If you will excuse me, I will return to Bracknell House and mourn my sister rather than spend another minute with gentlemen spreading tawdry gossip."

"She was involved with them," Rupert confirmed, wincing as he met Sanderson's incredulous expression. "I'm sorry. I shouldn't have kept the truth from you. I will return home as soon as I can."

Once Sanderson was out the front door, Rupert turned on Beecroft. "Who sent you?"

A smile curled up Beecroft's mouth, and then he laughed softly. "You know."

Rupert searched his mind. He had not seen the man who had saved him but he'd felt safe with him. *Relieved.* It was as if he should have known from the very beginning of the trouble who had helped him. He remembered short dark hair, olive skin. Tenderness. Familiarity. Spanish and Italian filling his ears.

Beloved.

His eyes rounded, and then he glared hard at Beecroft. "Say it."

Father stood, glancing between them. "What's going on?"

Lord Beecroft grinned widely. "I was utterly wrong and gladly admit it. Forgive me, Lord Bracknell. Imagine that. She's not dead after all."

"Yes, you certainly were wrong." Rupert burst to his feet, instantly regretting the rash action. He pressed a hand to his ribs and started the long, careful shuffle toward the door, ignoring his Father's suggestion to sit down again. Father sometimes fussed too much. "Take me to him. Now."

CHAPTER NINE

"You're looking well, Mr. Knight," Angelo said to his helpless prisoner after removing the gag from Knight's mouth. He was growing bored with his own company, and the banker's glowers too. He was pleased Victor Knight had recovered from the fright of his situation and for some time had ceased attempting to free himself.

Knight licked his lips and squinted at Angelo. "You're looking very much alive, Angela, and decidedly male, I see. What should I call you now?" Knight asked oh so politely.

"It hardly matters." Angelo shrugged. He'd worn many names, none dearer to him than the one given at his birth. "You could be dead soon if your beloved doesn't hurry up and return."

"And you're handsome," Victor Knight said, squinting, ignoring the jibe about his love life and the threat. "It really is an astounding feat the way you can change your looks to become anyone. I would never have known you if I wasn't already tied to this chair and staring down the barrel of a pistol you were said to own years ago."

Angelo grinned at the weapon and set it aside. He moved to a mirror, checking his reflection, and then scowled. He dabbed at the remnant of peach stuck to his lapel. "Yes, I tend to dress to suit the occasion."

This suit of clothes, however, stuck out like a sore thumb next to Victor Knight's quiet refinement.

"Where have you been?"

Angelo ignored the question. He flittered about the apartment, examining Victor Knight's belongings with envy. He missed the finer things in life. His little attic room was nowhere near as comfortable as the one he'd had at the Hunt Club.

He found a small kitchen behind a closed door and shrieked as he inhaled a much-loved scent. "Proper bread!"

He hugged a loaf of fresh-baked bread tight to his chest and inhaled the mouthwatering scent. Victor Knight had so much he couldn't possibly consume it all by himself.

Knight laughed. "If that had been a new club member you were drooling over, you even sound the same," he called out loudly.

Angelo poked his head from the room. Victor Knight was not taking the threat to his life seriously enough, if he was grinning back at him. He was bound, held at gunpoint, abandoned to fate. Had Angelo softened so very much that he was no longer threatening?

He probably wasn't today. He meant the man no real harm. Knight was a sensible man, not one given to brawling or belligerence. Beecroft liked Lord Bracknell, and would use his information and connections to ensure he was no longer under suspicion. The Hunt Club code of honor dictated he lie to save a fellow member, too.

Even so, Angelo had already chosen his exits, so there was no current danger he couldn't anticipate or escape, should Beecroft turn on him.

Angelo relaxed a bit then fluttered his lashes. "A man's nature never really changes."

Victor Knight laughed heartily. "Indeed, yours does not. I almost choked the first time you did that to me."

"That's why I do it. The members of the club are so easily bored that a little provocation lifts their spirits. You all like the challenge of something new and very different to conquer." After a few minutes more of rooting around, he started heaping food onto Knight's dining table for a feast. "Only the best," he murmured, mouth salivating at the choices before him, and dug in.

"There's wine in that cupboard over there," Knight offered helpfully with a tilt of his head to send him in the right direction.

Tavern food and ale were all very well but he remembered finer times with fondness. He found the bottle of French brandy and a fine glass to drink from. "For a man who's tied up and helpless, you certainly are in a good mood."

"I know Beecroft well now. If I were in the slightest

bit of danger, he'd never have left me alone with you. He wants to help you, and so do I. He has always regretted what he was forced to do."

"And yet he still shot me," Angelo grumbled around a slice of soft buttered bread.

"He said the pistol was yours, and contrary, bound to miss. Did he hit you, after all?"

Angelo scowled, remembering his shock at being fired upon with his own weapon. "Yes, of course he hit me, a wide shot but still—it's the principal of the thing that sets a man's teeth on edge."

"And you clearly did not drown in your terror of water," Knight continued.

Angelo regarded the man balefully. Not many knew that fact about his past. His family had been drowned, tied down by rocks and left to dangle just beneath the surface of the pond he'd swum in as a boy. Their deaths had led to his choice of career. How much had Beecroft shared about his past with his lover? "He knew my feelings about water."

Knight nodded. "He felt very bad about that. He told me what happened to your family all those years ago. The way they drowned. So terribly cruel to them and for you to find them that way. He said the channel was the only viable avenue for your escape."

Angelo heard the approach of a single man on the stairs. Heavy footfalls—but far too heavy to be Beecroft's lighter tread.

He spun out of the chair, retrieved his pistol and eased back toward a window he could escape through.

When Beecroft appeared, he couldn't understand why he'd not recognized his tread.

"It is done," Beecroft promised.

"Good, now—" Angelo began.

Bracknell stepped into the room and their eyes met.

And held.

Bracknell was the first to speak. "Where the hell have you been?"

Angelo blinked, wondering why the man sounded so angry. He had his alibi. His reputation was saved. Surely he'd been happier without Angelo around. He lowered the point of the pistol. Like Beecroft, Lord Bracknell posed no real threat to him. "Here and there."

Lord Bracknell still had bruises to his jaw, his arm was strapped to his chest in a sling, and he held himself a little too carefully to be in perfect health. Angelo glanced away as his conscience gave a twinge and noticed Beecroft had already untied Mr. Knight and was urging the banker toward the open doorway.

"Where the hell are you going?"

Beecroft smiled. "We won't return until tonight."

"Thank you," Bracknell murmured as they moved past him, but he did not leave.

Angelo stood frozen, a rare state. He did not know what to do now around Bracknell, a man he'd loved, and loved to torment about as much, but in another guise. He wasn't wearing a pretty gown or even fine clothes. He was as bare of tricks as he'd ever been.

Bracknell limped across the room, pulled Angelo tight against his chest with one arm and held him close. As close as any lover might after a long separation.

Angelo's breath caught as the familiar scent of clean male filled his lungs. The need to get close to Bracknell's hard body flared. Skin to skin, man to man. No tricks, no teasing. Honest lust and enjoyment of it.

Something the earl knew nothing about.

"I missed you," Bracknell complained against his hair.

Angelo shoved him away roughly. "What the hell is this?"

Bracknell cursed, holding his ribs tightly with his good arm. "Damn that stings. Did I hurt you too?"

"What?"

"The blows you took at the fight." Bracknell backed up a little, pointing to his body. "There was one blow to the ribs here that enraged you. Does it still give you pain?"

Angelo's breath caught. So he'd been recognized, but had it been before or after the beating? "What fight?"

"The night you saved my worthless hide from certain death in the back alley of Kirkland's hell. Beecroft lied about being with me. But you were there, fighting. The *Spaniard*. I couldn't tear my eyes away from you that night, and now I know why." Bracknell caught Angelo's face gently, titled up his chin to study his features. The look in his eyes was compelling, and then he smiled warmly. "This way suits you better. No more disguises. No more hiding who you really are."

"You're a fine one to talk." Angelo turned away abruptly, unnerved by Bracknell's proximity and mood. "Pretending to be happy to see me when that couldn't be further from the truth. You always say one thing but mean another."

Bracknell sighed. "I never believed Beecroft had killed you. I never gave up hope. I am happy, and I know I shouldn't be."

Angelo turned around, shocked. "Did you arrange her death, after all?"

"You know I couldn't have any reason to want her gone."

"She was unfaithful. An embarrassment." Angelo shook his head. "Did your wife turn to other men out of spite after she found out about your penchant for trousers?"

"Sally was unhappy with me for a long time and it had nothing to do with anyone else. I've only recently become aware of the extent of her unfaithfulness though. I do not condemn Sally for seeking the comfort I couldn't give her." Bracknell drew closer. "Thank you for sending Beecroft with your alibi. That's twice you've saved my life now."

The thanks grated. Saving Lord Bracknell had been a dangerous impulse he should not have acted upon. The more people aware he lived, the greater the chance he'd be pursued. "I suppose you'll claim to be wounded by her death. Faithful till the end, were you?"

"I *was* faithful." Angelo scoffed at that suggestion. "I took my vows very seriously," Bracknell promised.

Liar. "So seriously that your hand found its way under my skirts the very day we met?"

Angelo remembered the day well, and how eagerly Bracknell had embraced him, kissed him back. It would most certainly have gone much further if Angelo hadn't had a cock hidden beneath yards of Indian muslin that Bracknell objected to holding in his pampered hand. If he'd been a real woman...nothing would have stopped Lord Bracknell taking what he'd so clearly needed.

"Say what you like. I was undeserving of her, and you." Bracknell approached and touched his shoulder. Angelo shivered as the caress continued gently and Bracknell slid his fingers into Angelo's short-cropped hair. "My only indiscretion."

Angelo shrugged off the unwanted tenderness roughly. "I doubt that." He said it meanly, but had no real proof of Bracknell's infidelity. It was just a feeling. A resentment that he'd never be chosen.

"I was a conflicted man when I met you, but that is no longer the case." Bracknell leaned against him and Angelo warmed all over. "Don't disappear again."

When Bracknell slid his arm about Angelo's waist and squeezed gently, all the air in his lungs burst out. Angelo was held, willingly. Bracknell had not been tricked into passion by a clever disguise this time.

Angelo was wanted as a man. "Shouldn't you be mourning your beloved wife?"

"I will. In my own way." Bracknell's hot breath caressed the side of Angelo's neck. Angelo shivered again, caught off guard by the earl's pursuit. "I can guess what you think of me but I have responsibilities I cannot shirk, even for you. If I turn my back to honor Sally's memory as society expects, will you still be here when I come back for you?"

"You want to see me again?"

"Very much," Bracknell promised, leaning down to rest their heads together. Shivers raced through Angelo as the earl continued to whisper against his ear. "Where have you been?"

"Lots of places."

"Good places I hope," Bracknell said.

"Not always," Angelo confessed.

Bracknell pulled Angelo tighter against him. "You could have come back to me. I would have protected you. Hidden you from Beecroft and everyone that might wish you ill."

Angelo stared up at the earl, puzzled by that claim. Bracknell had only ever tolerated Angelo's presence at the Hunt Club. They were not friends, but his words rang with sincerity. He would have helped Angelo if he'd but asked.

There was at least four inches' difference in their heights. Bracknell, being so much broader, dwarfed Angelo. Around Bracknell, he had always felt small, uncertain, even nervous. His stomach, the most reliable of organs for sensing danger, quaked at the heat of Bracknell's stare. "I would never have asked," he admitted.

"Of course." Bracknell nodded, but then pushed against Angelo until he took a pace back into the wall. Pinned, held captive, his heart began to race. Ordinarily, he'd never allow such treatment. If it were any other man, he would be writhing on the floor in agony by now. However, since it was Bracknell, and he was injured, Angelo allowed it. He could easily break any hold the earl tried to put him in. He was dangerous for a reason.

"Where will I find you?" Bracknell's whisper sent gooseflesh down his spine and made his cock thicken. If Bracknell noticed the hardness against his thigh, he made no issue of it for a change.

"You can't find me." Allowing Bracknell to visit him at the boarding house was a very bad idea. They were already suspicious. Bracknell's presence in the Seven Dials would put them both at risk. "Don't come looking for me. Don't try to find the men who hurt you either."

"Because you dealt with them that night?" Bracknell asked but it was clear he suspected the lengths Angelo had gone to to protect him.

Angelo nodded curtly.

"All right," Bracknell agreed. "We will do this your way but only if you promise to return to me."

Angelo had been inside Bracknell's London home uninvited many times over the last few years, but of course he couldn't know. First, he'd gone to drink in familiar sights and smells, once to borrow a new warmer coat and a few coins when he'd been on the verge of starvation.

And once he'd snuck all the way upstairs to view the man's newborn child.

Lord Bracknell's young son had been left in the care of a negligent nursemaid, and Angelo had stood beside the crib for a good half hour, playing with the restless child who'd awoken in the middle of the night and gurgled up at him with no fear. The child was the spitting image of the man he loved, and so precious he'd had trouble tearing himself away. He'd left that night the way he'd come in, with no one the wiser that he'd invaded uninvited.

Bracknell brushed his thumb across Angelo's split lip. "Does this hurt?"

Angelo shook his head.

Bracknell lowered his head farther and kissed Angelo hard.

Angelo rose to his toes before he thought better about what he was doing. It had been a long time, five years or more since their last kiss. A long time to go without the touch of pleasure. And he was feeling it now. Bracknell knew what he was about when it came to kisses. Angelo quaked, caught up in desires he'd firmly pushed aside.

He drew back, staring at the man looming over him. How deep did Bracknell's change of heart really go? Would he finally give in to temptation, wish to become Angelo's lover?

Angelo was done with settling for half a love life. If Bracknell were in earnest he'd have to prove himself. "Leave the east window in the study unlocked after seven. If I'm coming, I'll be there before ten at the latest."

Bracknell sealed his lips to Angelo's in a kiss again that left him weak at the knees and scrambling for his wits. The earl cupped his face as they kissed, seemingly a very changed man. Angelo caught the earl's hips and drew him closer. Hard cock met hard cock with only fine wool and rough canvas between.

The earl drew back quickly. "I'll wait until midnight every damn night," Bracknell whispered, exasperation in his voice.

Angelo slid along the wall to put space between them. "I am sorry about your wife's passing."

Bracknell inclined his head. "So am I. Don't forget, I'll be waiting for you for as long as it takes."

CHAPTER TEN

Rupert paused at the doorway and then paced into the room where his wife's broken body rested. Sally had been covered by a sheer black cloth and roses had been scattered all about her still form. He felt uneasy that Sally had been dead for so many days and he'd not known. The scent of rose and death made him pause, but he curled his fingers into his palms until the moment of weakness passed and forced himself to move forward again.

He must do this. He must say goodbye. Forgive her, and ask for her forgiveness too. He had not loved her the way she had deserved, and after today, he knew why that hadn't been possible.

He'd been blind, ruthlessly ignoring his own needs out of duty. Duty to his family, the title, society's expectations of gentlemanly behavior. He should never have married Sally, even if he'd done so because he needed an heir. He had not been fair to her, and he hoped she'd never sensed it.

He paused at her side, noting Sanderson was in the room, staring at his sister from a chair near the wall, the tracks of tears shed on his shadowed cheeks.

"She always loved this room," Sanderson whispered without looking his way once.

"She did." He stared at her face through the veil, and he swallowed hard. "We held our wedding breakfast in this room with our family and friends looking on."

Sanderson hadn't been present for the wedding. The once joyous occasion was now a dim memory for Rupert. He'd felt such hope for his life then, for himself and Sally.

Sanderson sniffed and then stood. "Do you know who did this?"

"Not yet. But I promise you I will find out," he vowed.

The man drew close and thumped his shoulder in a show of solidarity, but thoughtlessly caused Rupert pain. He held in an oath as the sting receded. He was still very tender in places.

Sanderson strode out without a backward glance, leaving Rupert to say his farewells in silence.

Sally was to be buried tomorrow in London. Entombed with her parents, as had been her brother's wishes. Father had made the arrangements while Rupert had been recovering from his injuries, and there was nothing he'd wanted changed or needed to do.

He sighed. "I'm so sorry, love. You didn't deserve to die like this."

Sally, of course, made no response.

He'd been told how she'd been found, not how she'd died. It seemed a fall was the most likely cause but... his experiences with Angelo Marinari had taught him never to take any situation at face value. He glanced down at his feet. "Was it only an accident behind your fall or was there malice involved?"

His wife had been seeing four men in the last year, two of whom were known to him, one he'd never met, and Lord Beecroft had mentioned a fourth mysterious party that had not been identified as yet. The two men he knew already had an abundance of witnesses who placed them nowhere near her body. But they had friends and other lovers. It may be suspicious of him but everyone was a suspect. The one thing he knew for certain about Sally was that she would never use the servants' stairs in any home unless it was burning down around her. Her lovers might have alibis but was it possible that someone connected to them had harmed Sally?

He understood why he'd been the first suspect. Sally had been unfaithful, and he'd known about her behavior for some time. If not for Angelo, he'd be in chains. At least now his name had been cleared, he could do some investigation of his own.

He brushed his lip with his thumb, thinking hard over possible situations that might have led anyone to wish Sally harm. He had not known his wife well these past years. She had a close circle of friends; most would have been at the Dunhill event. If he spoke to them now, after being a suspect himself, would they tell him the truth of his wife's life or try to keep her secrets from him still?

A throat cleared, startling Rupert out of his thoughts. He turned to see the butler, a man Sally had brought into his home, edging into the room. Needham's eyes were suspiciously moist. "Forgive the intrusion, my lord, but there are many at the door who wish to pay their respects."

Friends or suspects? They were all the same to Rupert today, and would be until he had the answers he needed. "Let them in."

He allowed Sally's friends access to his home, and accepted their condolences in his drawing room. But he watched their every move, every gesture, as they viewed Sally's body in the opposite room—weighing and considering what he knew of their relationships with Sally.

Almost all voiced concern that he had been the first suspect in her death. Time would heal his heartbreak, they said. He was saddened by the loss but not unbalanced by grief with Sally's passing. He would recover. He had too many people relying upon him to indulge in the luxury of falling apart.

A heavy hand settled over his shoulder. "Son," Staines murmured as the last of the callers drifted out the door.

"I didn't see you arrive, Papa." The front door closed with a loud thud and he shivered as the sound carried through the whole house.

"Understandable." Father put his arm around him, resting his hand on his upper arm as he'd done when Rupert had been a boy. He wanted to lean into his father, but he fought the impulse as emotions swept over him.

But those emotions were not the ones he was supposed to feel today. He felt enormous guilt over being happy for Angelo's return and growing anger that someone had denied Sally the chance to be happy too.

Father sighed. "I lost your mother when you were young too. Don't do to Charlie what I did to you. Don't turn away from those who love you in a bid to hide how you feel."

Had Rupert been as much in love with Sally as his father had with Rupert's mother, his warning might have been needed. Father had turned to opium and his addiction had once driven a wedge between them. "I won't," he promised.

"Did you find the person you hurried off to meet?"

Angelo Marinari, stripped of feminine fashions and very much alive, was a revelation. The man was not the same character he'd met years ago though. The flirt he'd known and expected to meet was gone. The years apart had hardened him, turned him into a man Rupert struggled to reach. "Indeed."

"And?"

"Whole and hearty. The same, more or less."

"You're being cryptic," his father accused.

"I'm standing ten feet from my wife's cold body discussing a person that once dressed as a woman."

This father blinked rapidly. "You saw Angelo?"

He glanced at his father. "Did you not guess who really saved me? I thought the conversation with Beecroft had made it very obvious, or perhaps I'd already begun to suspect it myself."

"Oh," Father said as his eyes widened. "Oh, that is good news. Of course, he cannot return to the Hunt Club anymore but still..."

"Obviously he cannot return to employment," Rupert agreed. A dead man wouldn't be safe even in the privacy of the club. Having Angelo return to wearing dresses and flirting with every man who walked through the door didn't appeal to Rupert either.

"We should do something to help him?"

"I already have," he promised. He'd slipped money into Angelo's pocket, without the man knowing he'd done it too. Enough funds to last him a month in hiding. That was as long as Rupert was prepared to wait to see the man again.

"Is he here?" Father paled, looking around quickly as if expecting the former assassin to jump out from behind a door.

"No, and before you ask, I don't know where he is now or when I'll see him again."

It had been quite humbling to accept that he must wait yet again to see Angelo. Rupert was almost certain the man lived near the spot where he'd been attacked. How else would Angelo have found him to rescue that night?

"How do you know you *will* see him?"

Because Rupert believed he would keep his word. He knew that Marinari desired him still. He'd felt it in his kiss, in the way he'd trembled under Rupert's fingers. Angelo would be back one day. "Because he said so."

"I don't understand," Father began, brow furrowing. "I thought you two didn't get along."

"We didn't," he conceded. Rupert hadn't liked the way they'd met, the way he'd been deceived, or the way he had acted when faced with the shock of discovering a man dressed as a woman. Angelo had certainly flirted like a woman. It had been an embarrassment then how he'd reacted. He'd certainly shocked himself well and truly, and Angelo had never let him forget it either. "But I do like him," he promised. "He was very helpful, wise almost, despite his behavior and other occupation."

"Angelo was wise?" Father laughed. "You must have known him better than I did."

"I suppose I did." After the first shocks, getting better acquainted with Angelo had changed him. Expanded his narrow view of the world. He no longer took anything at face value; he no longer returned the smiles of pretty women. "Redding told you what happened when we first met, didn't he?"

"He said you figured him out faster than I did."

"Faster and more directly," Rupert answered. "In the guise of Angela, he almost lured me to break my vows. Is that definitive enough of a confession for your taste?"

"But I thought..." Staines frowned severely. "I thought you had, but not with her. With other women, I mean."

"I did my duty to Sally, Father, and to the family. I tempered my desires the only way I knew how. Abstinence," he bit out harshly.

"Oh Rupert, you shouldn't have needed to do that. I never meant... I always hoped you and Sally were happy together." His father sighed. "I wish you had told me of your struggles. Not all marriages are happy ones. Your mother and I sometimes squabbled," Father confessed. "The ups and downs of the past seem so inconsequential these days."

He studied his father, a man who'd been involved in at least two scandalous duels in his life over lovers after mother's death. Abstinence had never been Father's way. Father might not have married again, but that did not mean the duke was in any way a saintly man. He took his pleasures where he wanted and to hell with the consequences. Rupert did not approve but he'd come to understand his father better in recent years. Father had been looking for love.

Right on cue, Francis Redding appeared, his father's new great love, holding Rupert's only son in his arms.

"One of us had to be respectable," Rupert murmured to end the discussion.

It pained him a little that his nature appeared to be very much like his father's. Yet he wasn't attracted to all men. But he reacted to one consistently. Angelo was a very dangerous man to be drawn to.

He moved out of his father's embrace.

Redding tickled Charles under the chin, grinning at the boy's squirming. "He was asking for you. I didn't think you'd mind if I brought him to you, now that everyone has gone."

Redding passed Charlie across into Rupert's safe keeping and he juggled his energetic son to a comfortable position on his hip. "How long must I bear the sling, Redding?"

"Another day and then see how it feels," Redding suggested. "Longer cannot hurt."

Redding pulled a stuffed toy from his coat pocket and then a cloth-wrapped biscuit from another. He handed them all to the boy, who thanked him sweetly, and, hugging the toy, began to nibble on his food.

Charlie was so good—a quiet boy by nature. Innocent. Rupert kissed the top of his son's head, his anxiety settling as Charlie hugged him back. This child meant so much to him. He was the future of the family and the only link he had left to his late wife.

"Can we see the horses?" Charlie squirmed, ready to get down and run, but Rupert struggled to hold on to him a bit longer.

His father danced at the edge of his vision, feet shuffling impatiently for a turn to take the boy. Rupert smirked but did not meet his father's gaze or hand over the child. He looked at Charlie instead. "Should we take Grandpa with us?"

Charlie nodded, stuck his thumb in his mouth and lay his head on Rupert's good shoulder.

Across the hall, the housekeeper slipped into a chair near his wife's body, keeping vigil.

Rupert turned away. There was no need to risk upsetting the boy by remaining here any longer. He was too young to understand what death meant and for that, Rupert was grateful. When Charlie was older, he would tell his boy of his mother's beauty and grace, her love of life. He'd never mention the rumors or malign her memory. "Off we go."

His father fell into step beside him immediately, a doting grandfather determined to lure the child into his arms and into trouble.

Charlie, however, had other ideas. He reached over Rupert's shoulder, hands stretching for Francis Redding. "Come on, Reddy."

Rupert smiled at how simple life was to a child, and let his son choose who carried him. Rupert's ribs were starting to ache again anyway. Charles swayed toward Redding while Father clucked his tongue in disapproval.

Angelo had once claimed that children were the best judge of character. Charlie obviously knew whom he trusted already, given the way he clung to Redding. He was loved and Rupert was reassured that those who loved him would protect him without question.

His boy was bound to get into trouble sooner or later with his grandfather's help. The pair were already sneaking tarts from the kitchen and making a mess eating them, but at least Redding would ensure the duke never got completely out of hand. Charlie would always be safe under Redding's watchful eye. Rupert had been when he'd been growing up.

They were an odd family, but there had always been love and the strength of unfailing support. They would survive Sally's death, and always miss her.

CHAPTER ELEVEN

The small room Angelo rented over Wiggan's boarding house reeked of boiling onions and harbored a faint underlying odor of the rear lane filth, thanks to the gap around his window frame. He rolled onto his side on his narrow bed, staring at the place he'd called home for the past half year, and had to concede he did not like it entirely as much as he once had. A few days had made all the difference. Thanks to his brief visit to Victor Knight's home, he was reminded there were better places a man could rest his head.

He deserved better.

Perhaps it was time for a change of scenery, something to shake off his dissatisfaction with life and his future. Or perhaps it was merely the rainy day dampening his enthusiasm for life. Although Lord Bracknell claimed to want to see him again, he was afraid to, and that was a ridiculous feeling for an assassin to ever have.

He bounced to his feet. He absolutely did not need to return to Lord Bracknell, no matter how sincere he seemed. Bracknell had somehow managed to slip money into his coat pocket without him feeling it, unwittingly providing Angelo with a vast array of options for his future. He glanced at the spot where he'd hidden the coins, safe from prying eyes and nimble fingers. He would certainly need those coins if he wanted to take up a new life elsewhere.

He would go someplace fresh where no one cared to know his unhappy past. Yes, a change of routine and outlook would be very good for his soul. Angelo had enough now to set himself up comfortably in a modest abode if he was frugal.

He glanced at his attire with a grimace. He was far too shabby to be seen out and about during the daylight hours of past haunts without drawing unwanted attention. He'd have to change, become someone else for a while, something he'd become very used to doing over the years in his line of work as an assassin. He could not risk drawing attention, and he must blend in seamlessly. A clever disguise always hinged on the use of a perfect name.

He would not take the name of anyone he knew in London. He would act a gentleman, but not a lord. Assuming any sort of fictitious title would make him far too memorable.

He began collecting the few things he had that meant something to him, putting them inside his shirt for safekeeping. Now to decide on a profession—something worthwhile, and yet not the sort of thing people might actually wish to engage with. A man who travelled for his living. Perhaps a—

"Spaniard!" Mr. Wiggan roared outside his door, and Angelo lost the answer.

His door rattled and then sprang open without warning.

Angelo faced the man, doing nothing to hide his surprise or displeasure at the interruption. He'd been just about to settle on his new career! "What is the meaning of this?"

Wiggan scowled at him fiercely. "You've got some explaining to do..."

When two cooks from Kirkland's gambling establishment joined Wiggan, standing just outside the door to block any escape in that direction, Angelo's heartbeat grew to a loud thud in his chest. On spotting blood on their hands and clothing, he turned to the window and threw it up for air, as he had frequently done around these two. The scent of blood never actually bothered him, but it bothered the Spaniard, and opening windows gave him a way to flee if needed.

He turned back slowly, lifting a scented handkerchief to his nose. "You've been at the slaughterhouse again. Gods, you stink of cattle entrails."

"I don't give a fig about your sensibilities," Wiggan warned.

A boat builder? No. He was only good at burning boats and he hated the open sea. "I'm sorry to hear that," he said, appearing pained.

"You were seen carrying a body." Wiggan slammed the door shut behind him, leaving his two companions outside.

Stupid thing to do.

Angelo could overpower Wiggan in an instant, break his neck, slip outside and disappear across the roofline before anyone knew what he'd done. He really did not want to kill a man who'd been kind—in his own limited fashion.

It was only an accusation so far. That was easy to manage and deny. He sat on the window ledge, forcing calm into his body but ready to roll out of harm's way if he couldn't talk Wiggan out of his suspicions. "Many things are seen in London but so few are true."

"I pay you to make me money, not bring trouble to my door."

"True. I've made you a lot of money," Angelo said with firm conviction. He'd made him so wealthy that Wiggan had once hinted he could retire to the countryside. "If the report of carrying a body happened to be true, surely you didn't want to keep a rotting corpse around? The authorities do not take kindly to murder."

"Did you carry away a corpse?"

"No." He shrugged, thinking quickly. "But I did happen to aid a drunk on his way a few nights ago. His snores were disturbing my rest. He was quite loud and persistent about it."

"His name?"

"No idea. One drunk looks much like another when he's drooling. He was very much alive when I left him." He cocked his head to the side. "I hope that will be all."

"There were three men found dead in the lane the morning after the last fight. Kirkland's new hires."

Angelo took a moment to appear to consider the matter before answering. "I don't recall seeing anyone about."

The tavern owner scraped his fingers though his sparse hair, his expression troubled. "Kirkland is livid. He wants the killer dead."

Angelo frowned at the news. Vendettas were so

tedious. "There've been a dozen deaths in that lane this past half year that you've never come to my door asking about. What difference could three more make?"

"One of them was Kirkland's nephew."

Angelo swore, but in his own native tongue without thinking, and then clamped his lips shut.

Unfortunately, Wiggan understood enough Spanish to frown at the unfamiliar cadence. "What was that you said?'

Angelo shook his head, appalled at his slip of the tongue. "A curse an old friend once used. It's not important."

A mapmaker! Yes, that would give him ample excuse for any nomadic wanderings and the need to return to London from time to time. Now for a dull name to go with the new line of work.

Mr. Higgins? No.

Mr. Hope? Yes. Hope sounded very good.

Mr. George Hope.

Perfect. Angelo had never been a George before.

Angelo rolled his shoulders, eager to embrace his new personality immediately. Every good illusion depended on how a man carried his body around the world. People reacted according to how he held himself. A mapmaker wasn't the sort of fellow anyone should notice and should have the most worn shoes of anyone. He slouched a little, making himself seem weaker. He needed to act deferential and just a bit unaware of other people.

Wiggan shoved his shoulder. "What?"

Angelo startled, wondering when Wiggan had drawn close enough to touch him. "I'm sorry?"

Wiggan took a pace back. "You rolled your shoulders. You do that movement before every fight."

"Do I?" Angelo remained in the window. Wiggan was too clever by far, or perhaps Angelo had simply stayed in one place too long. No one should know him that well.

Wiggan glanced around, suddenly sensing his vulnerability. There were just the two of them in a small space, and Wiggan knew what he could do in a rigged fight without breaking into a sweat. The man took another pace toward the door and placed his hand on the doorknob.

Angelo sighed heavily. "You're a good man, Wiggan."

Wiggan shouted for his men even as Angelo rolled backward. He fell with fluid grace borne of years of practice and landed on his feet on the adjoining building's slate roof. He balanced on the slippery shingles a moment, listening to the sounds of confusion from above.

"After him," Wiggan demanded.

"Time to leave," he muttered to himself.

A ball from a pistol shot shattered the tile beside his left foot and he flew forward, moving quickly out of range of the weapon. He balanced carefully as he traversed upon the slick ridgeline of the next thatched roof and then jumped across a wide gap over a narrow lane.

He turned after landing safely on the next roof, one of slate this time.

Wiggan hung out Angelo's attic window, shaking his fist and shouting. Wiggan's men were struggling to find their feet on the uneven roofline between them.

Angelo bowed grandly as one of the men pursuing him fell through a weak point in the thatched roof with a scream of panic and pain. He bid Wiggan goodbye. Angelo had trod this path a dozen times or more and knew exactly where to place his feet to avoid falling through.

He leapt from building to building; heading toward obscurity that could only be found among the river folk, and then slithered down to firmer ground.

He stole a hat to keep the rain off his head and shoved his hands in his empty coat pockets before he swaggered off down a road, apparently without a care in the world or in any hurry. He grinned at his near miss and then his smile died. He'd failed to retrieve his full purse before being uncovered by Wiggan. Without money, he might starve.

He couldn't go back to reclaim his property so he did what he knew best. What he'd done at sixteen. He picked a pocket or two along the way, enough to hail a hack, and then headed toward the only dry place of safety he could count on sneaking into in this weather.

CHAPTER TWELVE

Rupert shivered as his wife was laid to rest in the St George's burying ground northeast of the city. He'd barely heard the words meant to offer solace on the loss of a loved one as they'd stood beside Sally's grave in the light rain.

It was done. He was a widow. A free man.

And yet he still felt himself bound.

He needed answers.

Rupert shook hands with those who'd followed Sally's body to the graveside, barely hearing their words meant to offer comfort. Sally had been well liked, and despite, or perhaps because of gossip, the gathering was vast, as was the number of pitying glances aimed in his direction.

He held his tongue and his temper but noted two of Sally's lovers lingered beyond the crowd of mourners, speaking with each other in low tones. He gave them a wide berth. Lord Deveraux and Lord Peterson had ironclad alibis for the night of her murder, so there was no point speaking to them.

Father drew close. "About the boy. I'd like to keep him until tomorrow."

Rupert nodded. "It would be best."

Father's hand settled on his shoulder. "I'll see you home."

Perhaps tonight Angelo would visit him at last. He'd expected the man yesterday, but despite remaining awake until two, and even opening the front door once, the man had failed to put in an appearance. He was becoming a little concerned that Angelo had run into trouble over the men he'd killed while saving his life. "There's no need to hover, Papa. My carriage is perfectly capable of delivering me home. There are some things I need to take care of first."

Father patted his shoulder again. "All right but if

you need company, I am always available."

"I know." He tipped his head toward the ducal carriage. "You'd best get back to Charlie before Redding becomes his favorite."

"We're not in competition with each other," Father promised before rushing off.

Rupert remained still at the graveside, staring at other headstones until everyone else had left. He glanced down then at Sally's fresh grave. His throat grew tight with emotion so he merely nodded one last farewell with a troubled heart.

He should miss her more, shouldn't he?

The gravediggers hovered at the edge of his vision, ready to lay down the mortsafe over the coffin and protect his wife's final rest from being disturbed by grave robbers. His heart grew heavier still when he turned and was confronted by Sally's lovers, Lord Deveraux and Lord Peterson, who now blocked the way to Rupert's waiting carriage.

"We will have revenge for her," were the first words out of Lord Deveraux's mouth.

Lord Peterson nodded, yet didn't meet Rupert's gaze. "Whoever hurt her must be brought to justice."

Rupert felt irritation at their assumption he felt any different. He didn't appreciate their suggestion he wasn't looking for her killer. "Indeed."

Deveraux drew closer. "What can we do?"

"I think you've done enough to tarnish her reputation." Rupert turned away from them in disgust to return to his carriage. He didn't need the help of these two scoundrels. If they'd truly cared about Sally, they'd have protected her from the accusations of their tawdry affairs and quelled any unsavory gossip about them.

There was a long silence behind him and then the pair fell into step with him. "Beecroft came to see us both, and we have realized something today about the unknown lover," Lord Deveraux whispered. "She was indebted to him."

Rupert paused and turned back slowly to stare at the so-called gentlemen. They had slept with his wife, and hadn't been discreet about the business. It burned to speak to them, but if these men had information he needed, he would have to. It did not mean he could like or forgive them, but he could not ignore them. "In what way and how much?"

"Not money, because I offered her more than enough for any extortion," Deveraux promised as he held up one hand. "She never said anything specifically, but when she spoke of her days away from us, she'd always cut herself off. I thought for a time that she was reluctant to speak about mistreatment by you. However, too many events happened when you were occupied elsewhere for me to continue to suspect you."

Rupert had hardly touched more than her hand or kissed her cheek in the last two years. That wasn't mistreatment but a retreat. He'd given up trying to woo his wife, but the suggestion she'd suffered at the hands of another appalled him. "What form of mistreatment?"

"When she was tired, she alluded to restrictions," Peterson added. "She spoke of a man but I don't think it was you, and it couldn't have been either of us."

Rupert glanced between the two men and then back toward the grave. To find Sally's killer, he might have to learn all the sordid details of her life. "So you were both her lovers."

"I was first, after your heir was born," Deveraux admitted. "It was a mistake. We were both lonely. After, we became good friends."

"Third," confessed Peterson with a grimace. "I would have taken her away if not for her fear of you."

"She couldn't have been afraid of me? Sally has been free to come and go at her whim since the day we married. I was never her keeper."

They regarded him warily. As if he'd an unpleasant side waiting to strike out. What the devil? They didn't trust *him*?

"When she would not welcome me back to her bed, I did not press my suit. I always let her make her own choices. Apparently that meant consorting with scoundrels of your ilk and abandoning her son to the servants' care."

Deveraux grasped Lord Peterson's shoulder hard. "I remember her talking of you. She said you didn't care."

He had cared, but with Sally, he'd felt out of his depth in recent years. He lifted his chin. "The birth changed her. She wouldn't stay still long enough to talk with me after the boy came along. I thought she simply needed time to adjust to her new role of mother. We never slept together after Charlie's birth."

The two men exchanged a startled glance. "Never?"

"Not even once," he growled.

"So you never had cause to leave bruises on her skin after going to her bed?" Peterson demanded. "Her arms often had marks."

"She bruised easily," Rupert agreed, thinking back over his conversations with Sally. "I am not the sort of man to take pleasure in another's pain. She always had little marks on her, since the day we met. She'd warned me about it before we even married. I treated Sally very gently because of that confession and even consulted her physician once. I forget his name for the moment."

"His name is Browne," Deveraux provided. "Your story will be easy enough to confirm. He is in town and I am sure he can be persuaded to speak with me, given the circumstances and the investigation. Assuming he can confirm your story about the bruises being a long-term affliction, then my money is on this unknown lover as our next point of investigation. Sally and I haven't been lovers for years and I couldn't have hurt her."

Rupert glared at Lord Peterson. "What about him?"

"Not him." Deveraux laughed softly, and then patted Peterson on the arm. "This one likes to be dominated. She'd tell him what to do and he'd obey like a helpless little puppy."

Peterson's face colored a bright scarlet and he refused to meet Rupert's eyes.

"She confessed to me not so long ago that she loved Peterson for making her life so easy when they were together. I had the impression the rest of her life was quite unsatisfying," Deveraux remarked, perhaps not realizing what he said was deeply insulting to Rupert.

"That was not my doing," Rupert promised. Who the hell had Sally been mixed up with and why had she never told him about her problems? It had been his responsibility to take care of his wife. "Someone must know. One of my servants might have information too."

"Agreed," Deveraux said. "That brother of hers might have some idea too, but I doubt Sanderson would share his suspicions when you're paying his bills."

Rupert grimaced. "Sanderson has been particularly angry since Sally's passing. I don't think he'll want to discuss anything that might tarnish her memory until he calms down. He's barely spoken to me since the insinuations that I was somehow involved."

"I have always gotten along well with Sanderson. Perhaps I could call on him at your residence and see what he lets slip when the past is discussed," Peterson offered.

Was Rupert willing to bring one of Sally's lovers into his home in search of the truth? At least no one could say he harbored a grudge after that event occurred. Rupert nodded slowly. "Don't push him. He's taken her death very hard."

"I'll of course be respectful," Peterson promised. "I did love her too."

Deveraux remained when Peterson hurried off.

Rupert met his gaze reluctantly. "Was there something else?"

"I want to apologize." Deveraux raked a hand over his jaw, appearing troubled. "Sally suggested you were completely unfeeling. I would not have come between you if I'd known the truth."

Rupert glanced away. "She chose to be with you rather than me, and there is no way I can forget that. If you don't mind, I'd rather be alone now."

"If you need anything, I'll come at once," Deveraux offered.

Rupert wouldn't ask, but nodded so Deveraux would take himself away.

CHAPTER THIRTEEN

It took a moment's work to pick the lock to gain entry to Mr. Knight's little apartment. He set his fingertips gently to the wood as he listened for movement inside. The door opened soundlessly with only the slightest of nudges.

Angelo drew his weapon and stepped inside.

"Ah, I hoped I'd see you tonight," Beecroft exclaimed rather loudly as he surged up from his place beside Mr. Knight's fire with a wide grin on his face and arms spread, showing he was unarmed. It was a little after eleven o'clock and the earl had been reading. There were papers scattered all about him that he hastily began to tidy up.

Angelo slid his lock-picking tools away in the pocket of his new suit and let the door close quietly behind him. "If you were hoping to see me, why lock the door?"

Beecroft gestured toward a far chamber shrouded in darkness. "Knight dislikes unlocked doors at home, especially after he retires for the night."

"And you oblige him in everything?" Angelo queried as he strutted into the room, allowing his new boots to strike rather more loudly than strictly necessary on the hardwood floors. There was no sign of Victor Knight, only Beecroft.

"I try to be a good friend." He gave Angelo a meaningful look. "And to be quiet while he sleeps.

"Friends?" Angelo snorted but softened his footfalls as he drew closer to Beecroft, but not within striking range. "A bit more than friends I should say."

Beecroft grinned quickly and sat down again. "I've missed you."

Angelo regarded the man he'd once answered to with skepticism and remained on his feet. "Why did you hope to see me? To finish the job?"

"No, no," he promised, proving it when he slouched

in the chair and crossed his feet at the ankles. Beecroft was more dangerous on his feet than settled on his bum, so Angelo relaxed a little. Beecroft reached down beside his chair and Angelo tensed again as he straightened. The earl revealed a rolled document. One with a seal affixed, if his eyes did not deceive him.

"This is for you," Beecroft said quickly.

Angelo stared at the document. He'd been given something of its like before, a secret commission to spy and kill for England, and his stomach pitted in disappointment. "I won't go back to that life."

"You misunderstand. I had a quiet word with my former acquaintances, and was given this in case you did. You are excused from all further inconveniences." Beecroft held out the document again, stretching much too far to have ulterior motives in offering it. "This is your freedom, my friend. Official."

Angelo crossed the room and, although suspicious, he took the document and inspected it. A royal seal held it closed and he pried it off the parchment. The paper seemed the right quality for an official government missive. He moved toward the nearest branch of candles to read the document in better light.

He sighed when he reached the end. It was about time. Freedom. Wealth. Thanks.

Everything he'd been promised at the start.

Angelo no longer had a need to live in the shadows.

He quickly rolled the document again and stuffed it inside his coat. "Excellent. Where is the money I am due?"

"You have an account at Hawke, Knight and Mumford. Mr. David Hawke, Knight's partner and good friend, will deal with you from now on."

"Hawke?" Angelo knew the name but not the man. "He knows about me?"

Beecroft shook his head. "Hawke knows nothing of your real past. You will have the new start you deserve. Hawke is under the impression you are a customer I brought to the bank and that the funds came to you from an inheritance. You had an aunt in Sussex who left you everything she had saved despite never having met you."

"How sad," Angelo whispered, and then he laughed. He

hadn't had a living relative in over a decade. His aunts were dead, drowned, as was everyone related to him.

"There should be enough for a house if you like, and a modest income from shares you own in a little mill Knight discovered in Kent last year."

A tidy fortune all round, and Angelo had a thousand things to do with the money. "How interesting that my aunt had the wherewithal to invest in a mill so far away from her home?"

"I had set aside the funds as a contingency in your name too. Just in case human decency failed upon your return and that promise was never kept." Beecroft shrugged and gestured Angelo to a chair. "It's the least I could do. I did shoot you."

He shouldn't stay but felt compelled to be sociable and sat down. "How have you been?"

"Oh, cannot complain. I'm glad I got out when I did. The business has changed since our days. The old guard is gone and thankfully more rational heads prevail. Lord Torrington in particular sends you his affectionate regards and best wishes for a long, happy life."

Angelo thought back a few years, trying to put a face to the name. "Ah, the man that blinds upon viewing at close range," Angelo murmured, remembering the spy hidden behind the bearing of a complete idiot. "Does Torrington still have an appalling taste in fashions?"

"He married, and I'm pleased to say his wife seems to have exerted some influence over his wardrobe. He's toned down his more garish attire so he doesn't always sparkle by candlelight quite as much."

Angelo shook his head and laughed. There were few in his profession who showed their true faces in society. Angelo had always preferred to blend in as much as possible. He put his hands on the arms of the chair, intending to stand and leave. "Well, if that is everything?"

"Please stay a little longer. I promise you are quite safe here," Beecroft begged, and Angelo subsided again. He already knew his exits from this room anyway. "Where will you go?" Beecroft asked.

There were so many possibilities, now that he had funds. "I don't know. Most likely I will leave London," he suggested. He'd never liked anyone knowing his whereabouts. But he had the good fortune of having already chosen a new profession to stumble about in for a while, attempting to appear to be making maps for a living if he wished to. He had a decent hand when it came to sketches and was eager to see a bit of the world too without leaving a trail of death in his wake.

And there was also the inconvenience of his recent kills to get away from. It was quite possible he was still being hunted through London's streets. He was more or less accustomed to that. How long any pursuit lasted would depend on how angry Kirkland remained about the nephew's death.

That was why Angelo still considered living under another name a good idea. Mr. George Hope had already stepped out into the world that night in his newer, finer clothing, courtesy of Lord Bracknell's tailor mistaking him for an errand boy, and he was confident his ruse wouldn't draw attention. Angelo glanced down at his new boots and conceded they looked *too* new. He'd have to scuff them well in the next few days. "There's nothing to hold me here."

Beecroft leaned sideways in his chair to rest his head against his fist. "Not even Bracknell?"

"Most definitely not." He kept his face impassive under Beecroft's scrutiny. Leaving before the mystery of Lady Bracknell's death was solved was the only irksome complication. He wanted to *know* the truth for his own peace of mind. He wanted assurance that her death had nothing at all to do with Bracknell. The man would never forgive himself if it had.

"Do you know he became quite worked up when I told him of your death? I thought he'd take a swing at me that day. Redding calmed him down, but we haven't actually passed a civil word since. He won't even acknowledge me at the club." Angelo stared at Beecroft until the earl grimaced. "You know he needs your help," Beecroft added softly.

"For what?"

"To uncover who killed his wife, of course."

Angelo gritted his teeth. He happened to agree with Beecroft's assessment. Bracknell had no nose for espionage. He took everything and everyone at face value. "Its none of my concern."

"He could use a man who knows how to reveal an unpleasant truth without gossiping about it. That man investigating, Forsythe, hasn't a clue what he's doing. I've been leading the fellow around by the nose since you came to me about the matter."

Angelo folded his arms across his chest. "No."

"Well, what else will you do with your life? Clearly your days of boxing as the Spaniard are done, especially after he's rumored to have killed three unarmed men."

Angelo blinked. Killing without permission was frowned upon by the higher ups. If they'd heard, Angelo would never have been pardoned. Everything he'd been granted could always be taken back. He only just resisted the urge to clutch his pardon for reassurance. "You believe rumors nowadays?"

"I may not be in the game anymore but my contacts keep me informed of certain facts. Sloppy work, my friend, but I can understand why it happened, and the provocation. The interested parties put a price on your head." Beecroft nodded. "But they have been appeased. You won't have any further trouble from that quarter whatsoever I promise you."

Angelo gaped. "Why?"

"You are my friend, you know," Beecroft suggested with a self-effacing smile. "How do you feel about living the life of an idle gentleman about Town instead of running away? It would be nice to have you around, for dinner and such."

Angelo let his hands fall to his sides in stunned amazement. Dinner and such? That almost sounded like a normal life. As a boy, his family had always entertained friends and neighbors at their table. They were some of the happiest memories he had retained of the time before he became an assassin.

Although he was a little disappointed that he didn't absolutely *need* to be a cartographer, he could choose that life still. But with no one hunting him, there was no incentive to keep this new identity. Staying in London *did* hold a certain appeal, but again, he would still need something to occupy his days. "Acting the part of an idle gentleman is hardly worthy or difficult."

Beecroft frowned, and then shuffled his sheaf of papers. "If you won't help solve the murder, what about becoming a tutor to Lord Bracknell's son instead?"

"Beecroft," he growled. Angelo regarded his former friend with renewed irritation. Dear God, he was a dog with a bone about Lord Bracknell.

"Why the hell couldn't you do it? You're fluent in languages and politics. The boy is the Duke of Staines' heir and will need all the help he can get to survive that influence."

Angelo laughed at that possibility. "The Duke of Staines is not a good influence on anyone. It is probably why Bracknell has become the way he is—the polar opposite of open-minded."

"I don't think he's quite as stiff as when he first came to the club. Still doesn't participate though," Beecroft told him with another indifferent shrug. "After what happened to the mother, young Charles might need a guard too," Beecroft added.

Angelo stiffened and curled his hands into fists on his knees.

Seeing his reaction, Beecroft winced. "Or would you rather be a substitute for his dead mother instead then? You could wear that pretty red silk gown you once favored. I heard Bracknell took your things home with him years ago. He might still have it tucked away somewhere."

Angelo struggled to hide his delight in the news that he could be reunited with his possessions. He'd never owned much at any time, but the red dress was soft and the buttons were solid gold. He'd never expected the earl to be sentimental...

And then he remembered Bracknell had worn Angelo's rosary beneath his shirt the night he was attacked.

Was there hope for Bracknell, and them, after all? To find out how deep the change had gone, he'd have to stay in London.

He snatched up Beecroft's papers and leafed through his notes. "I'll see what I can do about this."

CHAPTER FOURTEEN

A week later...

There was too much silence.

Rupert reached for his wine glass and took a small sip to wash out his mouth. He'd lost his appetite lately and tonight's meal had left a slightly unpleasant aftertaste. He pushed the food around his plate and choked the buttered asparagus down.

Dining with only Sanderson's company was damned uncomfortable business. Even the servants had begun to creep about the place as if disturbance of any sort was unwanted. He glanced at his companion, who was digging heartily into his veal.

Perhaps the food was fine after all, or was he sickening? Perhaps the aftertaste was only in his imagination, as so many things of late had been. He could swear he was losing his mind, along with pieces of clothing from his wardrobe. Distrusting everyone was wearing him down.

He took another sip of wine, covertly watching his companion in silence. Rupert had never noticed before that he and Sanderson only had Sally's comings and goings in common to talk about over dinner. Now she was gone, he didn't have a clue what to say except to talk about the investigation or speculate about her secret lover.

He couldn't do that with the footmen lining the walls and listening. He held his tongue and his brother-in-law remained sullen and pouting still. Not that Rupert blamed him entirely but damn it all, Rupert had lost Sally too.

He glanced toward the dining room door and freedom with considerable longing, hoping to catch a glimpse of Angelo sneaking in at last. He'd been waiting on the man too long and he was becoming concerned that Angelo might have left London after all. He had considered sending a note to Beecroft but decided against it. Angelo had demanded he stay away, so if Angelo wanted to see him, he knew where he lived.

"Are you expecting someone?" Sanderson asked suddenly.

"No," Rupert promised, returning his attention to finishing what he wanted of his meal. There was just the dessert course to come, and then he could escape Sanderson's stare. "Are you going out tonight?"

"How can you suggest it? I mourn Sally properly."

The little digs that Rupert hadn't cared about his wife were growing tedious. "I thought you might have friends to call upon." Rupert sipped his wine again. "Sally would not have wanted you to turn your back on them."

"How would you know what she wanted or not?" Sanderson exclaimed as he burst to his feet. "By your own admission, you say you hardly knew her."

Rupert set his fork aside and brought a napkin to his lips. "You're right. I didn't really know everything about her in recent years. But she loved you. She would not want you to wallow like this."

"It's only been two weeks."

The front knocker sounded and Rupert jumped.

"Thirteen days since she died," Rupert corrected him. "Eight days since we buried her."

Sanderson scowled. "When is the boy returning?"

Rupert gestured the two footmen forward to clear away their plates, impatient to learn who had come to call. "Charlie is having a holiday with the duke."

"I want to see him."

"There is nothing stopping you from visiting him."

Sanderson never left the house these days. "His mother would want him living with his father and not given away," Sanderson grumbled.

"He is with his grandfather," Rupert said, rising to his feet. "He is happy, I assure you."

"I should be looking after him. I am his guardian," Sanderson exclaimed with considerable heat.

Rupert's skin prickled. "How do you know about

that?"

The man frowned. "Sally promised me I would be when the boy was born. Did you deny her even that concession?"

"No." Father and Francis Redding were to be guardians to his son too, of course, but also Angelo Marinari was listed. Not that Marinari knew about the matter yet. Rupert needed to confirm the legality of the name he was currently known by to be sure it was the right one, and that his decision would stand up to any scrutiny in the courts. "The business of my estate is a complicated matter," Rupert reminded Sanderson, just as the butler tapped on the dining room door.

Rupert invited him in quickly to head off further discussion. "What is it, Needham?"

The butler's face was an unhealthy shade of crimson. "Forgive the intrusion, my lord. A Lord Peterson has called and wishes to know if he might have a word with Mr. Sanderson," informed him. "If you prefer, I can turn him away."

"Send him—" Sanderson began.

"He may stay," Rupert said, cutting Sanderson off quickly. About time Lord Peterson showed up. Rupert was starting to think he would have to send for him. "I will not rudely turn away a man I've learned was a friend of my late wife's and yours. There's enough gossip without creating more by being rude. I'll speak to him afterward, and alone."

Sanderson nodded slowly. "Thank you."

Rupert turned back to the butler. "Show Lord Peterson into the drawing room to await Sanderson's pleasure."

Rupert moved to a window as Sanderson stalked out, clearly angry about speaking to his friend, now that he was known as Sally's lover too.

Rupert stared outside into darkness, more worried about Marinari's current whereabouts than the lack of success of the investigation. Of course, an assassin could take care of himself, but still...anything could have happened to him and he'd never hear about it.

With too much time on his hands he paced the room, delaying putting in an appearance in the drawing room so Lord Peterson could talk to Sanderson in privacy.

Another knock sounded on the door. "What is it now?" he grumbled.

Needham entered promptly. "The tutor has arrived, my lord."

Rupert shook his head. "What tutor?"

Butler handed over a calling card.

Mr. George Hope,
Tutor and Translator.
London

Rupert blinked.

"The fellow asked me to say that you discussed employment the night the papers reported your wife's murder. He has delayed calling out of respect for your loss."

He looked at the card again, intrigued by the man's affront and real motive for calling. George Hope? Rupert's memory was perfect now and he didn't remember meeting any such person, but would prefer to appear in control.

He nodded slowly. "I remember something of that," Rupert agreed. "Very well, I will meet with him in my study since the drawing room is occupied."

Needham shook his head. "The drawing room is empty now, my lord."

"Peterson has gone?"

"Yes, my lord. He must have let himself out when I slipped down to the cellar."

That was unfortunate. He'd have to seek out Peterson tomorrow to discover what had been talked of. "Very well, but still show Mr. Hope to my study. I have some papers to attend to after he's gone."

Rupert waited a little while then strode to his private domain. He quickly shut the door behind him, ready to dismiss this imposter.

A neat gentleman wearing wire-rimmed glasses and elegant clothes stood before the fire and stared at him with one brow raised. Mr. George Hope was Angelo Marinari in bookish disguise. The clever bastard might look every inch a dull and proper instructor but Rupert's heart leaped out of his chest at the sight of his familiar face.

"How do you do?" Rupert strode across the room, hand extended for Angelo to shake as if they were new acquaintances. Rupert's heart gave a happy flip as their palms slid together and held. "Hope, is it?" he whispered.

"Indeed."

They shook hands. Marinari released him but glanced toward the closed door as a heavy thump sounded in the drawing room next door. He shook his head. Whatever Needham was doing in there wasn't important. Angelo had returned as promised.

Angelo was frowning though. "I was afraid you might not recall our prior meeting, my lord? Please accept my condolences for your recent loss. I was quite shocked when I read of the tragedy that has befallen you in the papers."

"Thank you. It has been a difficult time," he promised, playing along with Angelo's latest ruse, drinking in everything the man didn't say. He appeared fit, prosperous now. There was no sign of the poor rags or bruises he'd been wearing at their reunion at Mr. Knight's residence. "Please have a seat. Would you care for a drink, sir?"

"No. I never indulge." Angelo sat almost primly, hands folded in his lap. He reminded Rupert of every teacher he'd ever endured in his youth. His unruffled composure made Rupert want to misbehave, drop a book on the floor, pour ink out the window, just to see if he reacted the same way.

However pleasant those little rebellions against his lessons might have been in his childhood, Rupert took a place behind his desk as if this really was a business meeting. He was anxious to extend Angelo's visit as long as possible too. What was the fellow up to by assuming this guise? Charlie was too young to need a tutor. He would play along with this game as long as it kept Angelo talking. "I am glad you have come about the position. I expected you days ago."

Angelo smiled then answered him in Italian. "Forgive

the delay. I had some business to attend to with some city merchants first. Shall we get down to the business at hand? Proving my skill in languages seems the best place to start if I'm to be the boy's tutor."

Rupert smiled. He'd excelled at languages as a boy and had always liked to listen to Angelo's curses in his native tongue. Rupert would quiz him in Italian. "I hope all is well?"

"I have been given my reward," Marinari murmured in the same language. "I am assured of freedom."

Did that mean he no longer killed people for a living? Did an assassin ever stop having enemies to fight? He hoped so. Rupert leaned forward eagerly. "You are at liberty now?"

"To do as I please, or not," Marinari replied in Russian as he stood and strolled to the door. He pressed his ear against the hardwood and listened a long moment before he shook his head, clearly puzzled by something he heard out there, but he returned to his chair eventually and smiled.

"What were you listening for? Is something the matter?"

Marinari's frown returned. "Forgive me. In my former profession, a man tends to become suspicious of every odd little sound he hears."

"Of course," Rupert agreed.

"About the position," Angelo continued in Italian as he hooked one leg over the arm of the chair and slouched. Angelo ran his fingers along his trouser leg, stroking the material with a pleased smile. "I understand the boy is very young," he said, smiling with smug amusement when he noticed the direction of Rupert's gaze.

Rupert's mouth ran dry as his face flamed with heat. Angelo stretched out his leg, pointing his toe. He was wearing very nice hessians, not over-polished but they appeared well made just the same. Although he finely dressed now, one day Rupert would have to find out where the man had obtained those dresses he'd once worn. But Angelo wouldn't give up all his secrets today most likely. He wrenched his attention higher to continue the interview. "Charles is a little over four years."

"I prefer to teach young children in the evening, speaking to them before bedtime."

"Only at night? That is irregular." He grimaced. "Most tutors I had as a boy drilled me from early morning until late afternoon."

"The child is only four, my lord. Mornings are for play and eating. The young are best able to absorb a language more efficiently if they have no other stimulus or distractions," Angelo informed him as if he'd proved it somewhere before. "Besides, it is the only time I will have free to tutor little Charlie."

A surge of disappointment consumed Rupert. "Any tutors I hire will be expected to live here."

Angelo appeared very surprised by Rupert's suggestion. Rupert had had plenty of time to decide how he wished to live in the last week. He wanted to see Angelo every day, as he'd done before at the club, but also to become companions in the real world too. If he wanted to pretend to be a tutor, then he must act like one and live under Rupert's roof. "What are you doing with your days?"

Angelo took a moment to answer. "I was recently left a small fortune by an aged relative, an aunt, and I have quarters to furnish."

"Where is it?"

Amusement curled Angelo's lips. "In due time."

That wasn't good enough for Rupert. Not now. "What happens when I return to the country or take the boy to visit the duke's estate? Will you accompany us everywhere we go?"

Angelo brushed lint from his trouser leg, a slight smile on his lips. "I could be persuaded to accompany you if given the right incentive."

Frustrated, Rupert scowled. Of course, money was always a factor in any negotiation. "How large an incentive do you require?"

"What I want comes with no value in coin, and only you can decide if you can meet my price." Angelo fluttered his lashes. The feminine gesture had exactly the same impact as it had before when the man had worn gowns. Rupert's pulse raced with utter excitement. "Isn't it frustrating to have to wait for what you want?" Angelo whispered.

Rupert paused before answering. Angelo had always wanted Rupert as a lover. He'd never doubted that fact. Yet taking that final step into passion with another man was no matter to rush into or take lightly. What if he disappointed Angelo? The man had far more experience than Rupert ever could, and he was also dangerous to have as an enemy. He could not lose this friendship if he failed to live up to Angelo's expectation. He wished to take things slowly, to be sure they could remain friends if he failed to please. That's why it was imperative that they live in closer proximity, to make sure being together was what Angelo still wanted after all these years. "I want you to be happy."

Angelo nodded slowly. "If you want me, you're going to have to meet me halfway."

"Yes," he said, gulping down his anxiety. Rupert rounded the desk to be near Angelo. "When?"

"I cannot begin tutoring until the boy comes home, of course," Angelo remarked with a brittle laugh as he stood too. He lifted one hand toward Rupert's chest, slid it under the ends of his long cravat and paused over the rope of beads lying against his skin. "You're wearing it again?"

"Always," he promised. "I expect Charlie to return tomorrow," Rupert assured him quickly, stretching out his hand to stay the man. He caught Angelo by the elbow and squeezed. "My father dotes on Charlie, as you might imagine. Getting him back, well, the duke has thrown up every possible delay he can think of to avoid the inevitable parting," he confessed.

"No surprise there," Angelo whispered, fingers inching beneath Rupert's waistcoat. His lips quirked again as he drew circles on Rupert's skin. "The duke never bothered to grow up, did he?"

"Not very much and only under sufferance, I think," Rupert replied, observing Angelo's expression when he did the same. He slowly pushed Angelo's coat aside and slipped his hand to the man's waist. There was a spark of mischief back in Angelo's eyes, reminding Rupert of their earlier friendship, along with something more.

Warmer.

He drew Angelo against him firmly and touched his face. Angelo's skin was rougher than when they'd first met, the stubble that rasped against his fingers jolting him. "How often did you have to shave before?"

"Very often," Angelo whispered in a voice grown rough. More seductive than ever. "It was necessary so I did it."

He cupped Angelo's head gently. "Along with many unpleasant things I imagine."

Angelo nodded briskly.

Rupert dropped his attention to the man's lips when he licked them. Rupert felt breathless. He was hard already. His cock had a tendency to do that shockingly fast around Angelo, which had bothered him in the past but not anymore. Tonight, though, it seemed a sign that he was where he should be. What Angelo had once sought from him, Rupert would willingly give tonight. "Where are you staying?"

A strange smile lit Angelo's face, and then he laughed softly. He glanced down and touched the outline of Rupert's cock. The touch made him gasp out loud but then Angelo stepped back to bow. "Somewhere close by, never fear. I'll know when the boy returns."

Angelo turned away.

"Wait!" Rupert called as he charged after him.

Angelo paused at the door and looked pointedly at his crotch. "Hold on to that until tomorrow night. Have a pleasant evening, my Lord Bracknell."

Rupert groaned in disappointment as Angelo shut the door in his face. *Bloody tease.*

CHAPTER FIFTEEN

Angelo returned to Bracknell's house not long after midnight. He did not use the front door, visit the earl's bedchamber, or remain in the guest bedroom he'd secretly taken over that week, but went immediately to the small cupboard door he'd noticed leading off the entrance hall as he'd left earlier that day.

He found what he feared he'd heard—and acted swiftly to protect Lord Bracknell's reputation.

He almost broke his back lugging poor unconscious Lord Peterson across Town to Lord Beecroft's residence for much needed help.

Lord Beecroft appeared almost pleased to see Angelo and Peterson at first, but then noticed the blood Peterson was unintentionally dripping on his precious carpets from a wound unwittingly reopened by Angelo's jostling.

After a moment of confusion over the circumstances leading to Peterson's weak state, a reliable physician was sent for and Peterson was moved to Beecroft's study to be tended to very quietly.

Only then, when dawn was approaching, was the possible new lead in Lady Bracknell's death dissected from every angle.

"Someone is seeking to frame Lord Bracknell for his wife's murder by attacking Lord Peterson, a man known to be her lover," Beecroft complained.

"So it would seem." Angelo agreed, making himself at home in Beecroft's desk chair. "A second murder, unsuccessful in this instance, would have brought the earl back under very harsh scrutiny."

"This is bad," Beecroft worried.

"It is," Angelo conceded, becoming annoyed with the whole business. He had better things to do than clean up other people's messes. "But I'll take care of it."

Angelo slid open Beecroft's top drawer, put his hand

inside and reached up. Beecroft came closer, frowning at what he was doing. The stiletto Angelo had hidden in the desk years ago fit his palm perfectly still. He retrieved it and slipped it into his right boot. "I'll probably need that now."

"You'll also need to act in an official capacity," Beecroft warned. "Torrington gave me some latitude when I saw him. I have reclaimed certain powers. Powers that can protect you too."

Angelo grimaced. "Protect the earl."

"For Bracknell then," Beecroft hunted him from the desk and scrawled out a note. "Carry this at all times. Send for me as soon as you have a lead."

"I already have a lead, I just need to figure out the motive."

"You already suspect someone?"

"Of course," he promised, which was only half true. He had a household of suspects to investigate. "The villain revealed his location when he attacked Peterson."

Beecroft shook his head. "You need to watch over Bracknell somehow."

"I already have a plan for that," he said. "Someone in the house attacked Peterson and then stashed his body, with the end result being obviously to implicate Lord Bracknell in that murder too. Put a man outside Lord Bracknell's house and watch the windows for my signal."

"I've already done so," he promised. "I'll be among them, too."

"Good, and thank you." Angelo stood as he heard the unmistakable sound of servants stirring in the house. He had to leave immediately before he was seen. "Question Peterson when he wakes and get him to identify his attacker. It was not Bracknell."

"How can you be sure he wasn't involved?"

Angelo smirked and moved to a window. "He was too busy flirting with me at the time to think about anything or anyone else."

Beecroft choked on a laugh. "I'm pleased to hear it. Does that mean you're staying?"

"Perhaps," he replied. He was certainly thinking

about it.

Beecroft scowled as Angelo opened the nearest window and swung one leg through. "I do have a key to my own front door," Beecroft complained.

"It's more fun this way," Angelo promised, preparing for the fall to the ground below, and then he dropped to the ground before any more indelicate questions could be asked. He landed with a hard shock that made his teeth rattle together. He might have to consider using doors in future, since the landing caused him to limp a few steps.

Assassins never did live to any great age. They didn't usually retire.

Make every moment count.

Angelo fully intended to do that. He swiftly blended into the pre-dawn foot traffic to return to Bracknell's home so he could begin his investigations. He glanced up at the sheer brickwork at the rear of the dwelling with resignation though. Maybe he could indeed stand to use a few doors more often.

He threw himself up to the nearest window ledge, pushed open a window he'd marked as having a faulty lock just as the servants began rushing about, covering any noise he might have made as he slipped through.

He quietly crept upstairs and into a guest bedroom far from the servants' staircase, locked the door and flopped on the guest bed in relief. Keys were damn useful things to carry about. Maybe he should ask Lord Bracknell for one if he decided to remain with him indefinitely.

He stared up at the canopy, considering possible motives for the attack on Lord Peterson, and discarded each one. What he wouldn't give to have known Lady Bracknell better now. So much could have been discovered and discounted if he'd wormed his way into her confidence.

His lack of information worried him. He had held something of his concerns back from Beecroft. He feared he'd pushed Bracknell into bringing his son home too soon.

Little Charlie might be at risk the moment he came through the door, and no child should be made to suffer for the misdeeds of their elders. There had to be a way to protect the boy and find out the truth too, and quickly.

He rested in his room until the servants went down to luncheon, and then poked around the earl's bedchamber in search of any damning correspondence. Finding nothing unexpected, he peeked into the adjoining room. The scent of a woman's perfume overwhelmed him, and he smiled. He had missed such delicate scents in the last years. Exploring the room would have to wait until tonight though. The little lord's return had stirred up the entire household, and Angelo quickly slipped downstairs and out through the servants' back entrance while everyone was fussing over the happy child.

He presented himself to the butler at the front door at precisely one o'clock.

Due to the poor timing of his arrival, Lord Bracknell was otherwise engaged. Angelo cooled his heels in the drawing room, troubled by the lengthy delay. There were several spots of blood on the earl's armchair, nearly hidden beneath an embroidered pillow. The chair faced the doorway. The *evidence* that Peterson was attacked in this room, probably from behind, would certainly have implicated Bracknell, but there was a chance Peterson may not have even seen his attacker.

"So you're the tutor?" a voice drawled.

Angelo turned slowly to regard a gentleman he'd glimpsed wandering about the house before. Sally's elder brother was a narrow-faced but unremarkable fellow with none of her prettier features anywhere to be seen. Dressed all in black, he cut quite a sinister figure too. He'd no idea why Bracknell kept him about the place still, but he suspected Bracknell had become a sentimental sort while he'd been gone.

He smiled warmly. "You must be the earl's brother-in-law, Mr. Sanderson. Mr. Hope, tutor of languages, at your service, sir," he said with a deferential edge common of a man of learning who hired himself out.

He held out his hand as Sanderson drew close. His was squeezed with more pressure than was necessary, and Angelo felt himself assessed and scrutinized. He made a show of wincing over the tight grip to reinforce the illusion of weakness. "My condolences on the loss of your sister. Lady Bracknell was a very beautiful woman."

Beautiful, but boring to a man of Angelo's desires.

"How would you know what she looked like?" Sanderson asked, studying him anew. "She had no interest in tutors."

"I never had the pleasure of making her acquaintance, but I did glimpse a portrait of a woman above the stairs when I came in, and assumed it was hers," he replied, and took a step back. "I apologize if I was wrong."

Sanderson's attention flickered over him again and, by the slight hardening of his eyes, with suspicion too. "You were not wrong."

"Again, my condolences," Angelo murmured, bowing his head deferentially.

Sanderson turned away. "She was light and grace."

Angelo hoped Bracknell would appear soon so he'd have no further need to speak to Sanderson today. But he would watch him. He would watch everyone.

Angelo heard footsteps on the stairs and glanced toward the door. Bracknell burst into the room, carrying his young child in his arms. The boy seemed much more interesting, now he was awake. Tousled dark hair, wide brown eyes like his father's—dimples on his cheeks when he smiled too.

He switched his attention to the earl, eyes lingering on Bracknell's full lips. How wonderful it had been to be pursued as he had last night.

The earl cleared his throat. "Good of you to come, Hope."

"A pleasure to be here," he promised the earl. And the pleasure would have been worth the long wait, he suspected, given the way Bracknell had responded to him yesterday.

"This is my little rascal, Charlie," he said by way of introduction as he tickled the boy.

Angelo held out his hand. "*Come si va*, Charlie?"

The boy giggled and caught his fingers firmly.

Sanderson scowled. "What did you say to him?"

Angelo spared the briefest glance for Sanderson. "I said hello."

"In what language?"

"Italian," he said, turning from Sanderson. He smiled at the child he was supposed to teach. "Children learn best by watching and listening."

His first lessons would be in the tongue of Angelo's birth, and then others as the boy gained proficiency. He held out his hands for the child. "If I may become acquainted with the child, my lord. I promise to be most careful."

"He doesn't care for strangers," Sanderson warned.

Charlie reached for Angelo despite that claim. Sanderson was too opinionated for Angelo's taste, and since the man didn't seem to know even a basic Italian greeting, he would use it from now on just to annoy the fellow.

Angelo juggled the boy and the child stared deeply into his eyes. Charlie smiled suddenly and then cuddled into Angelo's chest with a contented sigh.

Angelo was delighted that the child might remember their past meetings and held him firmly, feeling entirely better himself. "It is good to see you again too little one," he told the boy in Italian. "But you've grown heavy this last year."

He glanced up as Bracknell began to choke. "Are you well, my lord?"

"*Si.*" A slow smile spread over Bracknell's face as he realized that Angelo had met the boy before. "What can I do to assist?"

Angelo knew the layout of the house like the back of his hand already, but for the sake of appearances, he probably should pretend to be clueless in front of Sanderson and everyone else. "If you would point me in the direction of the kitchens, I should like to make myself known to the household staff. Charlie and I will likely be wandering about the place a great deal, and I should like them to understand what we are doing if they do not comprehend other languages."

Charlie lifted his head. "I'm hungry," he said politely.

"Sì, naturalmente, a little tea and biscuit is a

wonderful idea," he assured the boy. Then he glanced at Lord Bracknell and noticed his amusement. The man had to stop grinning like that or he'd get a kiss for his trouble. He gestured toward the staircase and the back of the house. "I assume the kitchens are in this direction and below, my lord?"

"They are," Bracknell said, finally coming out of his daze. "If you will follow me."

Angelo carried Charlie after his father, holding him securely against his chest. He didn't have to look behind to know that Sanderson was watching them walk away without inviting him.

He could feel the man's cold gaze like a knife sliding between his ribs already. He didn't like Sanderson, and he would discover why as soon as possible.

CHAPTER SIXTEEN

"What do you know of this Hope fellow?"

Rupert folded the day's paper. It was an hour after the evening meal and he should feel on top of the world, but instead felt rather unsettled. Charlie's return and Angelo's arrival had distracted him at first, but he was again suffering an upset stomach. "I know enough," Rupert promised.

"Where does he live, what references did he possess?" Sanderson queried, putting his brandy glass aside.

Any references Angelo could have presented him with would have been undoubtedly false, so of course Rupert hadn't bothered to ask for any. All that mattered to Rupert was that Angelo had returned, earlier than he'd anticipated, and he had shown an instant rapport with Charlie.

His belly cramped suddenly, and he struggled not to wince at what that boded for the remains of his night. "His address is sound and his references are exemplary."

Besides, if Angelo had wished his child harm, he'd apparently had plenty of opportunities to do so in the past. It had been pretty clear they were already well acquainted before their proper introduction a few hours ago. His son went to Angelo with absolute trust, and Angelo seemed quite familiar with the boy, and Rupert's household too. Save for the introduction to cook, the man had charged ahead with his own instructions and had moved smoothly into his new role of tutor as if he'd always been one.

Rupert would find out just how often Angelo had visited his home in the past years eventually. His answer might reveal what had happened to his missing clothing too.

He set the paper aside on a nearby table. He hadn't

seen or heard the pair for a while and was keen to hunt them up. He didn't want to give Angelo a chance to slip away before they had another private talk. There was so much he needed to say to Angelo, and promises he wanted to make about the future.

He stood just as another cramp gripped his stomach, and he nearly curled over. He took a moment to recover and then slowly straightened, but a sweat broke out over his brow at the effort. "I'm on my way to look in on them now."

"I'll come with you," Sanderson insisted, regarding him keenly as he stood up too. "I say, are you quite all right, Bracknell?"

"It's nothing," he promised, brushing past Sanderson. "I do not require your company."

"I'm not worried about *you*," Sanderson claimed as he followed Rupert to the door.

"I know what's best for Charlie." Rupert faced his brother-in-law but struggled to appear dignified as heat swept over his skin. He had to leave the room, and he was tired of the man following him about so much. "Perhaps it is time you returned to your own life now. Do not feel you must remain in London to jolly my spirits along. Charlie and I will do very well, I assure you, and of course we do look forward to seeing you at Christmastime as usual."

He turned away, striding out of the room before Sanderson could call him back.

At the top of the stairs, Rupert turned into the bathing chamber and lost his last meal in the chamber pot. Gasping afterward, he cursed the timing. He could not afford to be ill now. He had Sally's death to understand and an old friendship to renew.

He cast up his accounts a second time.

He staggered out to the hall a good hour later, aware the answers he sought would have to wait until he felt more himself. He was going to take himself off to bed and trust that Angelo would return tomorrow.

The house was very quiet and he passed no one on his way to his bedchamber door. After entering, he noticed light spilling under the connecting door to Sally's former bedchamber.

He'd done nothing about her possessions as yet, but had ordered the room closed up, curtains drawn and door locked against idle intrusion. He was unaccountably annoyed that a servant or perhaps his housekeeper had disobeyed him. He was nearly too weak to do anything about that fact but shout at whoever it might be.

He dragged his feet to the door, grabbed the handle, and fell through when he pushed. He staggered a little, but his heart beat wildly when he discovered it was Angelo lounging across the curtained bed on his belly, with his booted feet waving back and forth in the air.

"What are you doing?"

"Keeping the boy company," Angelo promised, pointing to the carpet. "He misses her."

Rupert moved to look on the floor beside the bed, using the bedpost as an anchor to hold himself up. Charlie sat in the middle of a pink silk gown that had once belonged to Sally, and scattered about him were some of his mother's most treasured possessions. Charlie pressed her hairbrush to his cheek and then picked up her hand mirror to stare at himself.

"Always be gentle, Charlie," Angelo murmured to the child. "Mama would want you to be a good boy. She abhorred meanness in men, open carriages, and lemon tarts, apparently."

Rupert eased into a chair, watching his son play with her things. He should have considered bringing Charlie here before, but he'd locked away any trace of Sally as if she hadn't mattered. Of course she would always matter to his son.

He pushed down his guilt and glanced at Angelo, who was leafing through a book. "How did you know about the lemon tarts? Have you been spying on her all these years? On me and Charlie too?"

"I wanted to know very little of Sally, for reasons you should comprehend but which proved an insurmountable problem, I feared, until I found these hidden away." He waved the book he was reading upward. "Her thoughts and opinions are all here in her journals."

"She kept a journal?" Rupert dragged himself across

the room, and eased onto the bed beside Angelo. Resting seemed a very good idea right now. "I never knew she kept one."

Sally's neat script filled every inch of the page, by the look of it.

"She didn't hide them very well," Marinari said as he turned the last page and shut the book so Rupert couldn't read any of it. "There were three spread about this room, but there might be more elsewhere that cover the early years of your marriage."

He held out his hand. "Give them to me. You shouldn't be reading them."

Angelo tossed the book onto the bed far from Rupert. "If she wanted you to read them, she wouldn't have hidden them. Besides, it is better that I read them than you. These three volumes are quite lurid in places. You would only be distressed by what I've pieced together tonight."

Rupert slid to the floor beside Charlie and pulled the boy onto his lap. "What did you find out?"

"A great many interesting things." Angelo stretched and turned Rupert's face back to his. He swept his fingers up to Rupert's brow, frowning and staring into his eyes closely. "What is wrong with you?"

"I must have eaten bad food recently," he confessed, shrugging off the mothering gesture. "I'm feeling better already."

"I'll make sure of it," Angelo told him. His gaze travelled over the room, a fierce expression growing there. "I promise."

Charlie wrapped his arms tightly about Rupert's shoulder and cuddled close. Rupert rocked him a little, and then gestured to the books beyond Angelo. "What does Sally say?"

"She mentions you on several occasions with varying degrees of praise or disapproval," Angelo murmured apologetically. "It is interesting how we regard your interests with so vast a difference. She was quite disappointed by your love of boxing and physical pursuits, something I approve of in a gentleman, but I was fascinated by what she had to say about the men she had dangling after her too."

Rupert's mouth grew dry. "Does she name them?"

"Some, but not all, unfortunately. Your wife struggled with her place in the world, Rupert," Angelo whispered, before reaching out to ruffle Rupert's hair briefly. "You are not to blame for the choices she made in the pursuit of happiness."

"I wish I could believe you," Rupert whispered back, almost certain his son had fallen asleep in his arms. He lowered the boy onto Sally's gown gently, being careful not to wake him, and collapsed back against the bed.

Rupert closed his eyes when Angelo took up another book. He was very glad the boy was asleep early. He wasn't feeling particularly better, and an uneventful evening and an early night was what he needed most. He idly wondered if Angelo would mind taking the boy up to the nursery for him, but then changed his mind. Charlie was his son. He would be the one to tuck him in at night.

Angelo's long fingers tapped the book suddenly. "Ah, there it is."

Rupert became instantly alert. "You have the name of her lover?"

"And from that name comes the most probable reason for her death," Angelo murmured as he rolled to his feet suddenly. He moved to the window and peered out. When he turned around again, he strode swiftly toward him.

He looked up reluctantly. "So it was murder?"

"Indeed it was," Angelo promised, sounding aggrieved as his scowl grew.

When Marinari did not continue his explanation, Rupert had to ask, "Who was he?"

"Someone she fretted was the true father of your son," Angelo said in a hard tone lacking any forgiveness.

Rupert gasped at that suggestion. "He is my son!"

Charlie woke and sat up, half-asleep at his side. He put his arm protectively about the boy.

"Oh, I believe you," Angelo agreed. "Sally was foolish in that regard. Unfortunately, I am not the one that must be convinced."

Rupert struggled to stand. He'd strangle Angelo if he

continued to withhold the name. "Damn it, Angelo, stop trying to protect me."

As he raised his eyes, he was confronted by his brother-in-law holding two pistols aimed at both of them.

He moved in front of Angelo to protect him. "What the hell are you doing with weapons drawn, Sanderson?"

Sanderson waved the pistols, gesturing them away from the bed. "You'd be wise to hand over the boy, Lord Bracknell," Sanderson demanded. "He *is* mine, after all."

CHAPTER SEVENTEEN

Angelo's temper simmered just beneath the surface, hot, dark, and deadly, as Charlie began to cry. The boy may not understand the words but the charged atmosphere in the room had unsettled him.

Such insolence. A pair of pistols? And with the child present? One pointed at Lord Bracknell. The other pointed at him.

Angelo longed to wrap his fingers around Sanderson's neck and squeeze until his face turned red then blue in death.

But he was badly positioned to attack.

He stood between Bracknell and Charlie, and the innocent boy must be protected at all costs until help arrived. The boy was too young to understand that he should run away to safety, so for now Angelo was rooted to the spot in order to shield Charlie from any accidental discharge of the weapons. He studied both carefully, and then suppressed a groan as he recognized the one on the left.

Where the hell was Lord Beecroft or that ineffectual investigator to stop this travesty of bad luck! He was about to be shot with his own weapon again.

He calmed himself, focusing on the situation. Bracknell was in danger but showing no signs of alarm. Angelo was rather proud of him right now. He'd deliberately put himself in harm's way to shield Angelo. "What do you want Charlie for?" Angelo asked of Sanderson.

"He's mine."

"Yours?" Bracknell exclaimed, his face turning red. "He most certainly is not yours. The guardianship does not come into effect until I'm dead."

"Death is inevitable," Sanderson said as he smiled and waved the pistols about. "Did you never see how alike the boy and I are?"

"You're his uncle. Of course there is some resemblance," Bracknell protested. "But that is as far as your connection to Charlie goes."

Sanderson's eyes shone with mirth.

"That is not what he speaks of," Angelo said as he took a pace forward to grasp Bracknell's arm and turn him slightly back toward the boy. "*He* is the secret your wife kept from you."

"No." Bracknell shuddered. "Not him. She would never have bedded her own brother," Bracknell protested, appearing even more ill than he had before. "How can you suggest such an ugly thing?"

"I don't believe they were brother and sister," Angelo whispered, tugging Bracknell backward a little more. "A distant relation at best. The similarities in their features are superficial. Eye color, hair that curls. Narrow lips." Angelo decided the man was at best a second cousin.

"I'm glad you know," Sanderson admitted, his grin sly and decidedly smug. "We played our parts so well, no one ever suspected we were not what we claimed to be."

Angelo saw movement in Bracknell's bedchamber and almost broke into a smile. Beecroft had come—and about time too. He signaled for Lord Beecroft to wait. He wanted a confession that would put an end to the matter once and for all. "Is that so?"

Sanderson grinned and lifted one hand. "By the way, thank you for bringing your own weapon to begin your new position. Quite bold for a miserably paid tutor to carry one about. But when I found it hidden in your great coat, I knew what I had to do. Bracknell's death will be so much easier to pin on you with this little gem of yours lying beside two cold corpses."

"You're going to shoot me?" Bracknell's tone was slightly raised in alarm. "But why?"

"Things were moving too slowly the other way, so a direct approach seems expedient. In commerce, there must be a balance between income and expenses. I am cutting out the middleman to ensure the profit to me becomes commensurate with my contribution. When you're gone, I will hold the purse strings and have control over the boy's life. Sally told me everything about the trust you set up. It was only right that you named me to care for him when you're gone. I can bring up the boy in the manner I see fit without your further interference."

"There are other guardians." Bracknell shifted, moving slightly closer to Angelo.

For a moment, a look of rage crossed Sanderson's face. Angelo couldn't have Bracknell harmed. He needed a clear run at Sanderson if he was to be of any use in stopping this nonsense before precious lives were lost.

He took a pace forward and discreetly waved Bracknell back toward his son. Bracknell should protect the boy. If Sanderson believed Charlie to be his, he'd never fire a weapon that might bring the boy harm. To Sanderson, he said, "What reason will you give the authorities for my actions today?"

Sanderson shrugged as if motive was unimportant. "The obvious. You were enamored of Lady Bracknell's beauty and when she naturally laughed at your professions of love, you took to following her about and killed her in a jealous rage."

Bracknell choked.

"She's dead, so what is my reason for murdering Bracknell now, and Peterson earlier?" Angelo asked conversationally as Bracknell gasped again. "That is Lord Peterson's body stuffed in the closet downstairs, isn't it? More of your handiwork, I presume?"

Sanderson at last appeared uncertain. "Indeed it is. Jealousy made you unhinged. You could not bear that she loved *them* and not you so you killed him."

"Ah, the oldest reason for committing murder." Angelo drew in a deep breath. "Jealousy and vengeance."

Sanderson's plan was rather full of holes though.

The first being his ignorance of Angelo's true nature. Angelo was decidedly against petticoats unless he was wearing them himself. Sanderson couldn't know his preference for men either. He'd no cause to become jealous of any woman.

The second, and by far the largest hole, was that he

hadn't checked to see whether Peterson had stopped breathing.

It was just a matter of time before the trap was sprung now. Angelo just needed one last piece of the puzzle to tie off the remaining loose end. He wanted to know how it began.

"She was very beautiful. Full of life, eager to please the gentlemen who vied for her favors. But did she love you? She had other lovers. Is that why you pushed her to her death at the Dunhill Soiree? Had she had enough of your stinking breath when you forced your way into her bed?"

Sanderson re-aimed Angelo's pistol at the center of Angelo's chest, his smile tight. "She loved me."

"She loved many men, but in her heart, she was loyal to Bracknell and her son. She did everything she could to protect them. She put up with you." Angelo had read the diaries, read of the lover that could not be turned aside, the awkwardness and threats of harm to her son. Sally had written more than once that she'd been trapped by a mistake, and soon became afraid of the harm that could come to her son. She probably had been afraid to end the affair with Sanderson—a man who would punish her for imagined slights, leaving bruises on her skin over many years. "You were lovers for a long time."

"It was always me she favored," Sanderson boasted.

That was not what Sally's journals revealed. Angelo took another step forward, his body tense, coiled tight, ready to spring. "You knew each other since childhood. What happened to her real brother?"

Sanderson's lip twitched in a half smile at his question. "What do you think?"

Angelo didn't know for certain, but he could guess. "I think you killed Sally's brother because he betrothed his sister to Lord Bracknell instead of you."

"She should have been mine, and that fool had no right to keep her from me."

Perfect.

One more step and Angelo would be in striking range. His flexed his fingers at his sides—but then staggered as Charlie suddenly grasped both his legs.

"Charlie, no!" Bracknell cried out.

Fuck!

He didn't dare glance around to discover how the boy had slipped past his father, but Sanderson did. "There's my boy. Come to your papa now."

Charlie sensibly hid behind Angelo's legs instead even as Bracknell pulled on the child.

"Leave him be." Sanderson's jaw clenched. "Come here, Charles."

Charlie held Angelo even tighter and resisted Bracknell's urging.

"Give him to me," Sanderson barked out, waving the pistols wildly, and then pointing them both at Bracknell. "Or he dies here and now."

Sanderson intended to murder Bracknell no matter what happened next, so Angelo had no better option but to seem to obey. He reached down for the boy, quickly pulled the stiletto from his boot unnoticed, and swung the boy up into his arms. Angelo settled Charlie firmly on his far hip, and switched the blade from one hand to the other behind the child's back. He would have to be quick so the boy never noticed.

He moved toward Sanderson so fast, the idiot didn't suspect a thing.

Sanderson turned the pistols away as Charlie and Angelo lunged forward. Angelo pressed the blade to Sanderson's throat until blood welled but stopped short of killing him.

The pistols Sanderson held barked out, but thankfully the balls stuck only the marble mantelpiece and mirror above, and none of the men rushing toward them either.

Lord Beecroft and a dozen men swarmed over Sanderson. The investigator brought up the rear.

Angelo slipped his blade back into his boot then jiggled Charlie on his hip as he began to fuss. He turned to Bracknell. "There, there. The bad man is no more." He passed the child to his father quickly. "Your son, my lord."

Bracknell stared at the boy's face, his suspicions obvious.

"Never doubt the boy is yours." Angelo brushed back

the child's hair from his cheeks. "He has your ears, not Sanderson's. Charlie is most assuredly your offspring—bound to one day break hearts and cause mischief, like his father before him."

"You could have been killed, you idiot," the earl protested as he held the boy close. "Again."

He shrugged. "And by my own weapon a second time too. I do not fear death."

"Well I do," Bracknell complained with some heat. "I couldn't have borne it a second time."

Angelo smiled broadly, loving the fact that the earl was so upset over him. "Perhaps you'd better sit," he advised, urging the earl and his son toward a chair.

He was calm as the hall door burst open and servants swarmed into the room. At their head was the butler Needham.

"My lord," the fellow gasped as he took in the scene.

"We are unharmed," Bracknell promised as he held his son tight to his chest. "My friend saved us."

"Friend?" All eyes turned on Angelo. "I thought he was a tutor?"

"Hardly," Bracknell said, smiling broadly.

More footsteps pounded toward the room and there was no chance to pretend he wasn't alive anymore. Frances Redding beamed at him but the look on the Duke of Staines' face was priceless—a mix of horror swiftly followed by concern that his family was safe.

Angelo felt included in that concern too, but he stepped back as the duke began to demand answers of his son. He'd almost committed murder again, not for king and country, but for something far more important. He'd always kill to protect the people he loved most.

He glanced down at Sanderson, where he was struggling against his captors, saw the blood on his shirt, and smiled. The man was whole but if he came near Bracknell or Charlie again, he'd finish the job, and no one would ever find his body.

"Angelo?" Bracknell called over the din of the Duke of Staines' unending questions.

"Still here," he replied.

The earl touched him, set his hand to his shoulder

and leaned upon him. "Are you all right?"

"Of course," he promised. When he heard his real name being bandied about again, he winced. "So much for continuing this new disguise," he complained to Bracknell. "It seems the time to come out of the shadows has arrived."

"It's for the best." Bracknell clutched his belly.

Angelo considered Bracknell's illness and glanced around at the household staff. Everyone appeared accounted for and in perfect health except for the earl. A potential cause for Bracknell's current state occurred to him quickly, and he spun about to face the butler. "Mr. Needham, I should like you to have every piece of silver, plate, bowl, and glass washed and dried twice. Anything that could come in contact with the mouth or fingers must be thoroughly cleansed. Also, please strip the linen from the earl's bed and send it to his estate for boiling."

The man frowned, glancing at Bracknell in confusion. "Why?"

"Lord Bracknell is ill, and since no other member of the household is, too, I should like to remove any possible traces of poison left about by Mr. Sanderson here."

Beecroft moved to search Sanderson.

Angelo gestured Francis Redding closer. "You're needed."

Redding took the protesting earl into the next room by one arm.

He addressed the investigator. "Mr. Forsythe, do you have sufficient witnesses to Mr. Sanderson's confession."

The man blinked at him and then glanced around. "Indeed I do, thanks to you and the earl. How did you uncover what he was up to so quickly?"

Angelo winked at the fellow. "A lifetime habit of suspicion and mistrust."

Beecroft took Forsythe aside to whisper in his ear. The poor man appeared stunned when Beecroft finished, and Angelo was strangely relieved to not have to say that he'd killed for a living once upon a time.

"How is Lord Peterson faring?" he asked Beecroft

when he stood with a flask in hand.

"Recovering well," Beecroft promised. "He was attacked without provocation. We're lucky he heard a sound and turned just in time to see the culprit before he was struck. It was Sanderson all right."

"Good. Good."

"If I might have a word, Mr. Marinari," Forsythe begged with a slightly deferential manner as he indicated to a corner of the room.

Angelo nodded.

"Only the facts relevant to this case, sir," Beecroft whispered to Angelo as he passed him by.

Angelo filled Forsythe in on what he had uncovered during the hours since his arrival, passed over Lady Bracknell's diaries with regret, and pointed out the most damning passages of her affair with the man claiming to be her brother.

"I never learned what happened to the true Mr. Sanderson, but perhaps a search of the house might uncover something more. I will begin the hunt tomorrow and let you know if I find anything of further use."

"Thank you," Forsythe said, glancing quickly around them and withdrawing his card. "You seem like a good man, and very good at ferreting out secrets. Would you be interested in working together again?"

"Perhaps." Angelo read the card and tucked it into his coat pocket for future consideration. Who knew what the future would hold for him and whether he'd be capable of living as an idle gentleman? He very much doubted he'd be satisfied now with the nomadic life of a mapmaker, so an occupation might still be needed. "I'll be in touch."

"Careful with that," Angelo warned as Beecroft sniffed the contents of the bottle. He carefully set it aside gently before scrubbing his fingertips on a cloth. The fact that Sanderson might carry poison with him worried him. "Are the other gentlemen Lady Bracknell was involved with in good health? Did Sanderson seek them out too?"

"They are all safe and well, as far as I know," Beecroft promised, "but I will check on Deveraux soon to be sure he's come to no harm since I saw him last."

"I am eager to have this matter settled and end any further suspicions against Lord Bracknell, who has been an innocent victim of circumstance and decidedly foul play," Angelo announced, glancing at the investigator with one brow raised.

"Have Sanderson taken to this address for further questioning," Forsyth said as he gestured to his men. "I've seen and heard enough to acquit the earl of any involvement in the matter of Lady Bracknell's death. You may leave what remains in my hands. He will be judged for his crimes and suitably punished."

"Thank you, Forsythe," Angelo said. "Please continue to keep Lord Bracknell informed."

Beecroft's lips twitched in a smile. "I'll need you to come with me, Marinari."

"No," Bracknell cried out as he burst through the doorway, Francis Redding hovering behind.

Angelo went to the earl and held out his hand. "It is all right. Simply routine questioning after an assignment."

Bracknell clasped his hand tightly. "Assignment?"

"Of course." Angelo smiled. "Lord Beecroft asked for my help with the investigation and the matter is now closed. There is nothing more you need to worry about."

Bracknell appeared unconvinced, which couldn't be helped. Reluctantly, Angelo was released. "When will you be back?"

Angelo searched the earl's face and saw something new there. Eagerness. He switched to Italian to answer. "Sooner than you can imagine, my love."

Bracknell's eyes glowed and then he schooled his features to be serious. "You never gave me your address."

Angelo laughed softly. He met Bracknell's gaze and winked. "I'm sure if you consider the matter a moment or two, you will discover why I never needed to."

CHAPTER EIGHTEEN

Rupert shut the door to the rose guest bedchamber, nerves still frayed from last night's ugly business. He felt well enough now to walk about but Francis Redding had placed him on a regimen of plain food and water for the next week, to give his digestion time to recover from the suspected poisoning.

He glanced about him, and then shook his head. How foolish he felt at not realizing Angelo had been living under his roof, and for quite some time it seemed.

He poked about the chamber, discovering all manner of pilfered items he owned. There was his missing dove-gray waistcoat, discarded over a short chaise lounge that belonged elsewhere in another room. How Angelo had managed to cart the large piece upstairs by himself unobserved was a bit of a puzzle, but where the former assassin was concerned, perhaps it was better not to ask.

The fact that Angelo had been spending some night hours close by caused him to grin. Angelo must feel at home here, safe, and that gave him hope that in a world gone mad, the assassin would always return to him.

He moved to a screened corner and discovered a jug of clean water waited beside a dry shaving brush, along with a razor. Rupert picked up the implement, found it sharp enough to make his thumb bleed. He stared at the blood as recent events caught up to him.

He leaned against the washstand. He could have lost Angelo, and Charlie too. He could have lost what he'd only recently found.

His reason to be happy.

He blotted the blood on his thumb with his handkerchief as the door opened and shut.

"Have a care, Bracknell," Angelo complained. "I have

seen enough of your blood spilled to last a lifetime."

"I never saw my own," Rupert replied, and raised his eyes to Angelo's. "Redding had me bandaged before I saw anything too ghastly."

The man grinned back. "What are you doing here?"

"It is my house," he said as he approached the assassin slowly. Rupert removed a key from his pocket. "Would you be interested in using a door in future?"

"I detest front doors." Marinari folded his arms across his chest belligerently.

Rupert stepped toward him and freed one of Angelo's hands from the stubborn pose. He pressed the key into his palm and closed his fingers over it. "Indulge me."

"Perhaps," Angelo replied but threw the key away onto the bed in a gesture that seemed full of pent-up energy, or was it nervousness.

Rupert was nervous too. "How was it? The questioning?"

Angelo shrugged and turned away. "A little different than before. I now have to account for my every action and decision. Beecroft is satisfied, and that's what counts."

"I never once suspected Sanderson of being Sally's lover," Rupert confessed. He wasn't in the least bit jealous, but his pride was certainly smarting from that discovery.

"Why would you suspect the man who was known as her brother?" Angelo asked as he moved behind the screen and filled the washbasin. "It was a ruse done very well and over a long time. They looked enough alike that no one considered his presence odd. I must say, for all his flaws, I approve of Forsythe. He is committed to seeing Sanderson hang."

"I apologize," Rupert blurted out.

"For someone else's misdeeds?" Angelo glanced over his shoulder with a frown marring his handsome face. "I hardly think you forced Sally to bring her so-called brother into your home. She could have told you of her troubles. You would have protected her. She put you in danger instead."

"I meant I apologize for putting *you* in harm's way."

Angelo shrugged again. "It wasn't my first

altercation, my lord."

"Don't do that." Rupert crowded Angelo against the wall. "Don't make light of what you did for me. You saved my life."

Angelo pushed back but Rupert didn't budge. "I saved Charlie from a lifetime of bad wardrobe choices under Sanderson's poor guardianship. Did you see that hideous waistcoat the imposter was wearing today? It looked very much like the one the prince regent wore to Lady Creswell's soiree a month ago."

Rupert caught Marinari's shoulder firmly. "When were you at Lady Creswell's home?"

Angelo winked. "When were you?"

"It was Lady Creswell's birthday."

"The lamb was excellent, wasn't it?" Angelo's lips quirked. "You should pay more attention to other people's guests. Especially old ones. I can manage a credible gruff gentleman when I set my mind to it. I think I'll be using him again in the near future."

Rupert held Marinari by the shoulders. "You're not done with disguises?"

"Forsythe offered me a part in his fledgling investigation enterprise, and I must admit, he tempted me to agree. He has a number of cases he cannot crack, which seems inevitable now that I've come to know his limits. I may even have occasion to wear gowns again in the pursuit of the truth, so I'm going to need that trunk of my clothing returned to me." Marinari nodded and then flittered his long, dark lashes. "Think I can still fool you in the red dress again?"

"Not now," Rupert said as he slipped an arm around the man. "I see you. Then and now."

Angelo set his hands to Rupert's chest and nodded. "I'm going to put my skills to better use solving crimes rather than making them."

Rupert's heart pounded with pride as he slowly pulled Angelo closer. "I know you will be brilliant at it. What do you intend to do about *us* now?"

"Is there an us, my lord?"

"Most definitely," Rupert whispered as he brushed his lips across Angelo's whiskered cheek. "I'll need your patience and a little instruction though," he confessed.

"But you've been with a man before," Angelo protested.

"How did you find out about—" Rupert groaned and met Angelo's amused gaze. "Damn, you didn't really know until now, did you?"

Angelo sighed and looped his arms over Rupert's shoulders. "A broad palate is nothing to be ashamed of."

"I was with a boy when I was a boy," Rupert confessed, holding Angelo's gaze with the seriousness the matter deserved. "It ended badly. Neither of us were ever comfortable around each other again, and then he died. I have always suspected he couldn't live with what we'd done. I felt..."

"Responsible," Angelo finished for him.

Rupert nodded.

"Then you carried a burden you didn't need to," Angelo suggested, and perhaps he was right. "Everyone makes their own choices in the end, and I'm not going to kill myself if you don't want me."

"I don't want to lose you again," Rupert warned. Knowing they could remain friends no matter what happened, or didn't, made Rupert even more curious about making love to a man. "I don't know much, but I will learn."

Angelo pulled his head down close to his. "You will learn anything you want to know from me."

Rupert shuddered, overcome with anticipation for his first lesson to begin.

Angelo dug his fingers into Rupert's hair and pulled his head back, exposing his throat. "You'll love what we do together."

Angelo kissed his throat, just under his chin, and Rupert groaned when he was released. Angelo had always talked, teased, and tormented Rupert. He felt differently about that now. "What will we do?"

"We'll kiss, nip, bump and grind against each other. I'll take you in my mouth until you come undone and you will crave my touch," Angelo promised. He turned Rupert around to face the room, brought one hand swiftly to Rupert's neck and held him by the throat.

Helpless, Rupert didn't resist.

"Never let a man near your throat unless you trust him with your life," Angelo warned against his ear. "Especially not a lover."

"But I trust you," Rupert confessed.

"Good," Angelo whispered hoarsely as he dropped his hand. "When the time is right, I'll take my pleasure in you slowly, deeply, until you cannot get enough."

Rupert shuddered and pressed back into Angelo, unbearably excited by the sensations the man evoked. When Angelo palmed his cock, Rupert gasped. He was hard, eager for the next phase of his life. "I love you," Rupert whispered.

Angelo pushed him across the room and onto the bed roughly. Angelo didn't immediately join him, so Rupert twisted to look at the man.

Angelo stood a few feet away, tears filling his eyes. He brushed them aside roughly. "I've been waiting forever to hear that."

Rupert dragged Angelo onto the bed and kissed him soundly. They wrestled around on top as Angelo spoke of what he liked, and the pleasures they could share together. As small as Angelo appeared to be, he was unbelievably strong and impossible to conquer. A hot sweat covered Rupert's skin and he was panting by the time he conceded defeat.

Angelo pinned him to the mattress on his back, holding his wrists firmly above his head. "I like to be on top most of the time," Angelo confessed. "We must be quiet now."

He unbuttoned Rupert's trousers without another word, freed his cock and stoked him until Rupert was biting his lips to conceal how much he enjoyed it.

Angelo moved back to strip, so Rupert hurried to remove his own clothes. He played with the rosary hanging about his neck while Angelo set his own garments aside with far more care.

He scowled at Rupert. "My grandmother's rosary should never come to bed with us."

Rupert slipped it over his head and set it aside on the nightstand. "You should have it back."

"No," Angelo disagreed, attention flickering over

Rupert's nakedness. Under the weight of Angelo's regard, he grew even harder. "I want you to keep it."

Angelo stripped off his shirt and revealed he wore a woman's sheer white silk chemise dotted with ribbons and seed pearl about the neck. But just beneath the garment, he noticed the scar of the injury close to his heart.

Marinari shrugged on hearing Rupert's soft gasp but must have misunderstood the cause for it given his next words. "Some habits are impossible to break."

"I don't care what you wear," he promised. He brushed his thumb over the old wound. "Keep it on," he whispered roughly as he drew Angelo onto the bed. He set his lips to the scar, wishing he could erase the past that had caused Angelo so much pain. "It will be like the first time we kissed."

Angelo fluttered his lashes, adopting the feminine manner that had so turned Rupert's head when they'd first met. "You like me this way?"

"I want you, no matter how you dress," Rupert promised, brushing Angelo's hair back from his eyes.

"Good, because—"

Rupert silenced Angelo by pressing one finger to his lips. "So much time has passed since our first disastrous encounter at the Hunt Club. This time I know what I want, and that's you," Rupert promised from the bottom of his heart. The mad, dangerous, irreverent Angelo Marinari had stolen his heart well and truly. He cupped Angelo's backside as they stared at each other, giving over his heart and soul with absolute certainty his love was in good hands. "I want you to make this your home. You'll have me forever if living with me, becoming part of my family, pleases you," he suggested, to be sure Angelo knew he'd won.

Fighting this attraction was beyond Rupert's power, and against his best interests.

He kissed Angelo swiftly. He was once a husband, but only now finally committed to love. "We can be together forever," he promised. "Nothing will satisfy me but you."

Angelo, eyes spilling tears, shoved a hand between them and caught both cocks in a firm, hard grasp. The silk against his cock was heavenly soft, but hot, and soon they were moving against each other vigorously.

He stared at Angelo as he spilled his seed, and then felt Angelo shudder and shake against him too a moment later. Rupert held fast to Angelo, his world once more steady around him.

"Forever and always," Angelo agreed with a wicked laugh that promised their night was far from over. "And repeatedly."

EPILOGUE

A year later...

"Good evening, Mr. Needham," Angelo exclaimed as he threw his travelling cloak over Bracknell's butler's outstretched arms. "I'm home," he shouted out.

"Welcome back, sir," the fellow said with a wide grin and jolly laugh. "It's good to have you back again."

"Thank you," he said. Angelo had quickly seen the wisdom of moving into Lord Bracknell's life and homes shortly after becoming his lover. Separation from the ones he loved had been impossible anyway, so he'd moved in and had never been happier.

Once Needham had wrestled the travelling cloak into a better position, Angelo passed over a heavy basket of fresh fruit. "I thought cook might be able to do something wonderful with these beauties."

The basket was almost overflowing with peaches he'd bartered from a small farmer along the road toward London. He'd paid a fair bit more than they were probably worth for the privilege of picking each and every one himself. They were perfectly ripe. He'd eaten two on his way back to London just to be sure.

Needham smiled a little more warmly. "I'm sure she could be persuaded to make a few pies from all of this just for you."

"More than a few I would say. Should be enough to feed everyone employed here too," Angelo suggested. He wasn't above spoiling the servants with surprise treats from the country if it meant they enjoyed their work for Lord Bracknell more. This was his home now, and he chose to be affectionate to everyone.

"Angelo," Charlie called out.

"You're late, sir!" Lord Bracknell complained as he hurried down the staircase, trailing after his son, who moved much faster than his father. "Charlie's been looking for you for days."

The boy threw himself at Angelo, so he swept the boy up and hugged him tightly. "I missed you too," he told the boy in Italian.

"I missed you more," Charlie promised, stumbling through the language of Angelo's birth. The boy needed more lessons. "Did you bring me anything?"

"Peaches," Angelo whispered. "Cook is going to make you something wonderful to eat later."

The little boy's eyes widened with excitement. "Peaches are my favorite."

"Mine too," Angelo promised, hugging the boy again. It was lovely to be loved again.

Bracknell drew close, smiling broadly. "What kept you?"

He set Charlie down on his feet and ruffled his hair but the boy stayed near, leaning against his leg as he so often did when he returned from a trip. Angelo moderated his words to protect the boy's impressionable mind. "The fellow had the gall to run away and hide from me," he complained. "Can you believe it?"

"How utterly rude," Bracknell agreed with a soft laugh. "I assume you did catch him in the end."

"I did, even though he hid on a fishing boat." Angelo shuddered, recalling the torturous chase across open water. He'd warned Forsythe that the next time he suggested a pursuit was absolutely necessary, he'd beat the man senseless.

Bracknell laughed. "Still having trouble with water?"

"Only when I see it," Angelo grumbled.

"Maybe you'd prefer to try navigating the *ton* with me instead."

"Never," Angelo shuddered dramatically, which made Charlie giggle. Angelo did sometimes follow the earl to balls and such in disguise, but he found little fun in the experience. He didn't know how Bracknell could bear all the simpering ladies and pompous gentlemen so often.

They might live under the same roof, but had their own lives. Bracknell mingled with the cream of the *ton* while Angelo chased criminals all over the countryside. He'd completely taken over Forsythe's little business in the last six months with the man's blessing. He'd even expanded the scope of work he undertook considerably, and had hired new men, some younger sons of titled lords, instead of solely relying upon street urchins for their information.

He kept Forsythe on for company, to handle the tedious cases of commonplace thefts, paperwork, and troublesome employees.

Bracknell grinned. "Hard to avoid the water when your pursuit went as far as Portsmouth."

"As far as the Isle of Wight, actually," Angelo complained. "The treacherous fellow stole a fishing boat to add to his other crimes against society."

A trio of servants hurried past them, including Angelo's newest hire.

Bracknell gasped as a large man passed them. "Isn't that...?"

"Willem, the man I fought against behind the Kirkland gambling hell the night you were set upon, has the makings of an excellent servant if given clear instructions," Angelo promised.

He had discovered Willem mucking out the stables of a coaching house this last trip, and in such poor condition that he couldn't ignore his plight. Willem had run afoul of men who treated him poorly again, and Angelo couldn't believe his poor luck. Willem had been trying to return home to Portsmouth and his family for some time. Angelo had pitied him and had carried him home on the back of his carriage, after throwing him into a horse trough first, of course.

"I trust you know what you're doing," Bracknell whispered.

Angelo nodded firmly. Willem's home hadn't been fit for pigs to live, and it was clear Willem's family, while happy to be reunited with their son, could ill afford the expense to feed the large man. He'd tossed the father a crown and promised to employ the brute there and then. "Willem, you will answer to Mr. Needham now. He'll show you where you will sleep and give you chores to do until I have need of you. Take that basket from him and carry it wherever he wants it taken."

"Yes, sir," Willem said with a bright smile as he followed the butler toward the servants' quarters.

Bracknell eased closer. "Fruit again?"

"You know we adore peaches most of all." He looked up into Bracknell's face and smiled, wishing they could kiss hello for once without worry for the servants seeing them. He dropped his gaze quickly to Charlie and ruffled his hair again. Pleasure would have to wait until the boy was asleep tonight, most likely. "I couldn't resist the temptation, as usual."

Bracknell patted his shoulder and urged him toward the stairs with unusually firm pressure at his spine. Definitely a bossy nudge. What was the earl up to tonight?

"You must be weary," Bracknell suggested as he picked up his son and herded them all upstairs.

Angelo sniffed his sleeve, not liking that he still smelled of the harbor town. "Not particularly weary, but a change of clothing is definitely in order."

Charlie went away with his nursemaid easily enough at Bracknell's urging and the earl accompanied Angelo to his bedchamber door.

Angelo sighed when he entered and tossed his coat and waistcoat onto the small chaise lounge. He was home. All of his things were strewn about the chambers exactly as he'd left them two weeks ago.

Bracknell shut and locked the bedchamber door then rushed across the room to him. He swept Angelo's into his arms and kissed him desperately, until Angelo felt the urge to undress.

The long wait for Bracknell's unrestrained affection had been worth every year of frustration and torment since they'd first met.

"I missed you," Bracknell told him as he steered Angelo toward the bed they often shared at night. Sometimes, Bracknell was even still lying next to him when the sun rose, but not too often. Angelo, always the first to wake on any day, always hated shoving his sleepy lover out before they were discovered in bed together.

He smiled at his lover, thinking wicked thoughts

that thickened his cock. "That thing you did last time with your tongue at my back door. I enjoyed that."

Bracknell threw Angelo onto the bed and pinned him down. "Damn it, you did, too. Nearly screamed the house down."

Angelo set his hands behind his head and grinned up at Bracknell. He loved to torment this man every chance he got. Life was too short to waste being delicate about desire. "Will you do that to me again?"

Bracknell removed his coat and rolled up his sleeves. "I will do better."

"That would be quite a feat," Angelo warned.

Bracknell unbuttoned his trousers and pushed them down, then pushed his shirt up, out of the way under his waistcoat. His cock was already hard and full, ruddy with the arousal that he craved. Angelo was dragged to the edge of the bed by his hips.

He would have gotten up to suck Bracknell, but the man clearly had other ideas. He unbuttoned Angelo's breeches, dragged them halfway down his thighs, and pushed his legs up into the air.

Angelo smiled. Maybe he would have his balls and hole licked after all. He did enjoy having the earl on his knees. "Kiss me there."

Bracknell shook his head, leaned sideways to a nearby drawer and withdrew a glass bottle that Angelo had filled with oil months ago and never touched again. "You'll like this better."

When Bracknell oiled his cock, Angelo bit back a desperate groan. The earl slid one slick finger into him, and then another and another, until he was stretched and desperate. Angelo bucked, gripped by need. "Finally!"

A teasing smile lingered on Bracknell's lips as he took his fingers away and grasped Angelo's hips. He butted the head of his cock against him, and then exhaled as he pushed.

They'd talked of this moment two weeks ago, but Angelo had not expected to be taken as soon as he walked in the door. But making love was the perfect way to celebrate his success, and he was pleased that Bracknell had taken the initiative in bedroom matters at last.

He lifted his feet a little higher just as Bracknell thrust in deeper. He took the crown easily, and then forced himself to relax, and Bracknell eased all the way inside him.

"My God, you feel wonderful," Angelo whispered raggedly as Bracknell's cock filled him. He had wanted this for so long that he had to wrap his hand around his own cock and squeezed the base firmly to cut off his own excitement.

"My God, you're tight," Bracknell groaned as he withdrew a little way. He began to thrust, short jabs into Angelo that made him squirm and nearly moan aloud. Despite Angelo's best intentions, he teased himself with slow pulls on his own cock. It had been a long time since he'd been in bed with Bracknell.

Too long since Angelo had been made love to by someone he cared about.

"I like a great many things you do to me, beloved," Angelo whispered as he flexed to take Bracknell deeper. "I love you," he confessed.

"I know," Bracknell promised as he leaned over Angelo, skimming his fingers over his quivering abdomen. Bracknell pushed aside the chemise Angelo always wore and tightened his grip about his waist. His smile was full of love and devilish as he pressed deep. "You're an extraordinary man. Dangerous to one's health."

"Not to yours," Angelo promised as the man withdrew. There were only two things Angelo wanted in life, and that was to feel wanted and to make Bracknell smile like this.

He quickened his strokes on his cock as Bracknell found a rhythm that drove him deep and true. Their thighs slapped loudly and they quickly quieted their passions so the sound wouldn't carry beyond the bedchamber.

"So good," Bracknell whispered roughly before he shuddered, slamming into Angelo as deep as he could go and collapsing over him.

Angelo eased away from Bracknell, forced him to his side on the edge of the bed and stood. He positioned his cock level with Bracknell's face. Angelo brushed his cock against the earls parted lips. Bracknell licked them, and then opened wide for Angelo's cock to slide inside.

Bracknell had developed a definite enthusiasm for sucking cock. Angelo no longer worried about an accidental bite in the heat of the moment and closed his eyes, savoring his vulnerability. Assassins usually made poor bedfellows, but Angelo trusted this man with all his heart and soul.

He began to thrust roughly into the cavern of Bracknell's eager mouth, knowing his release was but moments away.

Today he wasn't having much success holding back his excitement. They'd been apart too long and he could still feel that he'd been fucked well and hard by the one he adored. He didn't have to imagine the sensation today, and there would be a next time soon he was sure. He moaned at the image of Bracknell pinning him down on his stomach, flipping up long red skirts and taking him from behind.

Bracknell caught Angelo about the throat suddenly and squeezed hard, making it difficult for Angelo to breath.

Instead of erupting in panic, as he would have with anyone else, Angelo bit back an excited oath and grasped his length firmly. Bracknell was dangerous in ways Angelo hadn't ever considered. The earl teased Angelo that he was the most stubborn bedfellow, always for fighting pleasure so it didn't consume his senses too quick. He'd easily discovered that Angelo loved to fight for everything, including his own release. He found being helpless, under Bracknell's control, both a novelty and wildly exciting.

He grasped the earl hard by the hair, and shuffled his hand up and down his cock rapidly. He spilled his seed down Bracknell's throat within moments with a strangled moan torn from his soul.

Bracknell eased him to the mattress as if he were made of glass and tucked him into the safely of his arms. He toyed with the beadwork on Angelo's chemise and sighed. "Better?"

Angelo looked up at his lover, his one great love, and his heart, once so used to disappointment, trembled at the joy shining in Bracknell's eyes.

"Everything is better when I'm with you," Angelo told him. "Never let me go."

"I could not now," Bracknell whispered as he rolled Angelo under him again and kissed him thoroughly. "We're making every moment count."

The End

ABOUT THE AUTHOR

Determined to escape the Aussie sun on a scorching camping holiday, Heather picked up a pen and notebook from a corner store and started writing her very first novel—Chills. Eight years later, she is the author of over thirty romances and publisher of several anthologies too. Addicted to all things tech (never again will Heather write a novel longhand) and fascinated by English society of the early 1800's, Heather spends her days getting her characters in and out of trouble and into bed together (if they make it that far). She lives on the edge of beautiful Lake Macquarie, Australia with her trio of mischievous rogues (husband and two sons) along with one rescued cat whose only interest in her career is that it provides him with food on demand.

You can find details of her work at
www.heather-boyd.com